P9-ECI-166

The Adventures of Midnight Son

The Adventures of Midnight Son

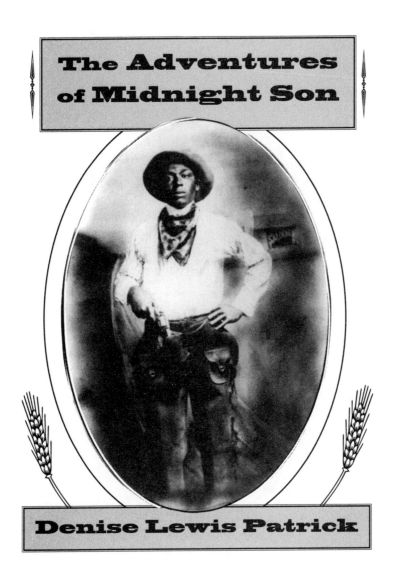

Denise Lewis Patrick

Henry Holt and Company ✶ New York

Henry Holt and Company, LLC
Publishers since 1866
115 West 18th Street
New York, New York 10011

Henry Holt is a registered
trademark of Henry Holt and Company, LLC

Library of Congress Cataloging-in-Publication Data
Patrick, Denise Lewis.
     The adventures of Midnight Son / Denise Lewis Patrick.
         p.   cm.
     Summary: After his parents help him escape from slavery
on a cotton plantation, thirteen-year-old Midnight finds
freedom in Mexico and becomes a cowboy on a cattle
drive to Kansas.
     1. Afro-Americans—Juvenile fiction. [1. Afro-Americans—
Fiction.   2. Cowboys—Fiction.]   I. Title.
PZ7.P2747Ad   1997   [Fic]—dc21   97-14406

ISBN 0-8050-4714-X

First Edition—1997
Designed by Meredith Baldwin

Printed in the United States of America
on acid-free paper. ∞
10 9 8 7 6 5 4

Title page: *Portrait of Black Cowboy Arthur Walker,* photographer
unknown. By permission of the Photographs and Prints Division,
Schomburg Center for Research in Black Culture, New York
Public Library, Astor, Lenox and Tilden Foundations

For all my brave brown cowboys:
Daddy, Austin, Kevin, Deryck,
Matthew, Dillon, Alexander, Jackson,
KJ, Kristopher, and Lance.

—D. L. P.

Midnight's Travel to Mexico
and the Trail Drive

*Became the state of Oklahoma in 1907

**Part of this territory became the state
of New Mexico in 1912.

The Adventures of Midnight Son

� decorative star symbols

WYANDOTTE COUNTY, KANSAS, was noisy, dusty, and wild. Horses and wagons crisscrossed over the main road. The new wooden sidewalks were lined with hotels and boardinghouses, saloons, and a bank. New buildings were going up all around. People were everywhere. There was plenty for a country boy to take in.

"Midnight!" When he heard his name, the boy turned his woolly head around to face the trail boss. Midnight wasn't like the others. He didn't hold out his hat as the money dropped from the trail boss's pouch. Midnight held out his big, dark hands.

One. Two. Three. Four. Sunlight bounced off each gold piece as it hit Midnight's sweaty palms. He felt them sizzle against his skin like fire. Quickly he closed his fist. "You earned every bit of that, boy." Joe B. spat out the words. "Never seen a cowpoke young as you work so hard."

Midnight couldn't speak. He nodded a thank-you and stumbled off toward the tree where his horse, Dahomey, was hitched. Dahomey nuzzled Midnight's tight hand, thinking there might be a goody inside for him. Sliding down against the tree trunk, Midnight paid no attention.

He carefully pulled a small burlap sack out of his shirt, opened his hand, and stared. The money seemed to melt into his skin and become part of him. That sizzling sensation went clear through his hand and shot up his arm. The feeling was like lightning, surging up from his arm to his chest. Then to his heart.

His heart thumped and flopped, then stood still. Midnight felt, for the first time, like a free man. He had money. Money he had worked for, earned fair and square. Free men bought and paid for what they wanted. Now Midnight, all of thirteen years old, was one of them.

A slow, steady smile began to spread across his face. He blinked and shook his head.

"Well, Dahomey," he said quietly, "what a free man does with his money is a serious thing." He pulled himself up straight and looked past a bunch of rowdy old cowboys as they circled around the trail boss.

About an hour later Midnight stood in front of Miss Ellen's Boarding House. As he stepped onto the porch, an old Indian man standing there beckoned to a water pump around the side of the building. Midnight frowned, then glanced down at himself. *What a sight,* he thought.

His shirt was stiff with red-brown mud. Mud was caked on his boots. His face and hands wore a thick layer of grit and dust. Midnight pumped water into a tin pail standing under the spigot and threw it onto his face. The dirt rolled off in a muddy stream. It had been weeks since he'd been anything close to clean.

There was a small, cracked looking glass nailed to the building. Midnight shook the water out of his eyes and stood up straight. In the mirror he saw a face looking back at him with two wide, charcoal gray eyes sitting above high cheekbones. A long, straight nose. A wide mouth. All set into a face the color of black coffee.

Midnight leaned closer to that mirror. It was his own face, all right. But how could he be the same? He'd been riding the trail for months, a real cowpoke. He jingled one hand in his pants pocket. The gold coins sang to him. He had money.

❋

5

How could he be the same Midnight Son who, barely a year ago, had left his mama and papa forever? How could he be the Midnight Son who, not long ago, had been on the run for his very life?

one

He had tried hard for a long time to block the past out of his mind. It just hurt too much when he remembered. But now, like the water splashing out of the pump, the memories came rushing forth in a flood. Everything, from the very beginning.

Midnight had been born a slave, just like his mama and papa. He was their first boy-child. Papa called him Midnight because he came into the world at the stroke of twelve on a hot Texas night. They said he was born screaming. His papa always said, "Sure 'nuff, you came here hungry. Had the taste of freedom in your mouth!"

Both his folks worked in the cotton fields on a small plantation. Midnight and six other slave babies were left alone on a straw mattress inside one of the tiny slave cabins. Hungry and wet, they lay for hours. Their mothers were only allowed to come and feed the littlest ones twice a day.

Midnight's six-year-old sister, Lady, would run out from her kitchen duties to check on the babies when she could. Sometimes she would bring a pan of leftover bread or biscuits and leave it in the middle of the dirt floor. The babies crawled over to eat out of the pan. At sundown, their tired mothers came from the fields to take them home.

Even as a small boy, Midnight wanted to get away from that dark room. As soon as he could toddle around, Lady taught him how to feed the chickens. When he was three he hunted for eggs in the chicken coop. He collected twigs and small bits of wood to start the big fires in the kitchen fireplaces. Then he pulled weeds from the vegetable garden until sundown.

Midnight's baby brother was born one morning when he was four. Mama was all smiles. Midnight and Lady kept peeping into the bed to see the tiny brown fingers and toes.

"We're gonna name our third child as good as we named the others!" Papa held Midnight on his knee. Lady sat on Mama's bed, rubbing the soft baby's cheeks.

"A strong name," Mama said.

"I know." Papa touched Mama's hand. "They say

back in Africa . . ." He looked down at Midnight. ". . . That's where us all come from. . . . There's this mighty water called the Nile."

"We'll call the baby Nile," Mama said.

"Nile." Lady nodded. Midnight clapped his hands. Mama and Papa laughed and laughed.

Just after Nile came, the plantation owner hired a new man to oversee the slaves. On his first day that overseer laid down a new rule: Slave mothers had only fifteen minutes to walk to the cabin to feed their babies. He rang the cowbell to signal a water break and rang it fifteen minutes later to start work again. If the women were late, he cracked his long bullwhip against their backs.

Now, it took most of that time to walk from the nearest field to the barn. The slave cabins were scattered uphill from there. Even if a mother ran to the baby cabin she'd never have time to nurse the baby and get back to the field.

Midnight's mother tried. She dropped her cotton sack and flew up the hill when she heard the bell ring. But Nile got sick when he was two weeks old. Mama stayed up nights trying to get him well. It seemed like Nile needed more milk and more loving than Mama had time to give.

One day Midnight saw Mama run by the garden to feed the baby. He stood up to wave, but she

✷

9

didn't see him. He watched her rush into the cabin, then he bent down to pull up a bunch of carrots. Before he could drop the vegetables into his basket, he heard Mama wail.

"Nooooo! Nooooo!" Her voice sounded loud and fearful across the whole place. Midnight couldn't move. It was the first time he'd ever felt scared. He saw Papa stand up way out in the cotton field. There was nothing Papa could do. He couldn't leave. Mama stumbled out of the cabin with Nile in her arms.

"My baby! My baby, he's dead!" she cried.

Midnight saw Lady run to the kitchen door, but the cook grabbed her apron strings and snatched her back. Midnight caught a glance at her terrified eyes. Then Lady was gone and Mama was still standing there. Alone.

That night, the slave owner let Papa bury Nile in an empty field behind the barn. Midnight watched Papa put the tiny wooden box in the ground near a shady bush. It was far away from the cotton field. Mama cried for days. Then she became quiet. Midnight couldn't remember ever hearing her laugh again.

Midnight missed his mama's laughing. He was only four, but he thought a lot about things. And he started thinking about that baby cabin. About Nile. *If Mama had been there, she would've taken care of him. But*

they made her stay in the cotton field until it was too late.
Nothin' like cotton should be more important than a little
bitty baby.

The family didn't talk much about Nile, or any-thing, after that. They just went on, day after day, working from sunrise to sunset. When Midnight was five, the overseer added tending the cows to Midnight's chores. He helped milk in the morning and herded them out to pasture before he went to the garden. In the evening he rounded the cows up and headed them back to the barn. Midnight loved that because those cows were so quiet and peaceful. He'd hum a little tune to them, and they would fol-low at his heels like puppies.

Midnight was walking out of the barn one cloudy fall morning. The owner of the plantation had died the week before, and everyone was worried about what would happen next. *Seems real quiet 'round here,* Midnight thought. He looked out at the field. It was empty.

"Get over here, boy!" A bearded white man appeared from nowhere and pushed Midnight around the corner of the barn. Every slave on the place was lined up in two neat rows. Midnight stared.

In front were the children. There was Lady, look-ing wide-eyed and scared. Behind were Mama and Papa. The man shoved Midnight. He stumbled into the line beside his sister. She grabbed his hand. Before they could pass words, the owner's wife came out onto the porch with a group of men. She nodded, and the bearded man walked up behind a tall wooden crate standing on end. He shuffled through some papers lying on top of the crate, then picked up a wooden mallet and knocked three times.

"Hear ye! On this day, the thirtieth day of September in the year of our Lord eighteen hundred and fifty-six, we commence the sale of forty black slaves from the estate of Lemuel Sampson!" He slammed the hammer three times again.

Sale! Midnight began to tremble. Lady squeezed his hand tighter. He wanted to look back at his parents, to touch them, but he was afraid. *Papa says masters don't care if they take black babies away from their mamas or black papas from their families. What's gonna happen to us?*

"Gentlemen." The Bearded one smiled. "We've got prime Negroes here. Well worth every dollar Mrs. Sampson is asking." He looked down at his papers and then up—straight at Midnight. Midnight sucked in his breath. He was afraid, like when Nile died.

"House slaves. First off—" He stepped away from the box and pulled Lady out of the line! Midnight tried to hold her hand tighter, but the man jerked Lady's narrow shoulder with such force that Midnight fell to the ground. Behind him, Mama gasped.

"—We have here a ten-year-old female, accustomed to serving in the dining room, experienced in general kitchen duties. Shows promise as a pastry cook." He spun Lady around to face the men, then banged his hammer.

"Bidding starts at five hundred dollars."

"NO!" Midnight yelled out, forgetting his fear. *They're gonna sell her! They're gonna sell my sister!* He crawled toward her in the dirt. "NO!" A shining black boot came down on Midnight's small brown fingers, crushing them. He raised his head with angry tears streaming down his face. It was the overseer.

"Get back with the rest of 'em, you little monkey. She ain't nothin' to you, 'cause you ain't nothin'!"

Those words rang in Midnight's ears like a thundering bell. He closed his eyes and wished he could disappear. Something inside him changed that day. It was like he lost part of himself. He never figured out exactly *what* it was, but he knew exactly *why*.

✳

two

Lady was sold to a man from Louisiana. They watched her ride off on the back of a wagon. Midnight and his mother and father were sold together as field hands to an older man called Greely. He set off right away to his cotton farm three counties west.

For Midnight and his folks, leaving the Sampson place behind was leaving Lady behind, too. The family's heart was gone. They couldn't speak her name anymore. They only had memories of her. Before, they had often whispered about being free together. Now that would never happen. They had to go on to another life without her.

At the new place, Midnight's two younger sisters were born. He missed Lady, but he loved Truth and Queen too. He started growing tall and strong. At first he did all kinds of chores in the barnyard and garden. Pretty soon Greely decided Midnight ought to move over to the cotton fields. So, between Mama and Papa, Midnight started.

They moved all day long with their backs stooped, picking cotton. Row after row. Pound after pound. The fluffy white plants flew from their fingers into the sacks they wore slung across their backs. Black women, men, and children spread across the flat land as far as anyone could see, picking and sweating.

Midnight hated that cotton more than ever. With every cotton boll he plucked, he felt like he was throwing away a dream. *I wanna see far-off places. Wanna own shoes. Have a gold piece, warm in my pocket. Wanna find Lady, wherever she is. And see Mama sittin', just sittin' and smilin', with nothin' to do for nobody. I wanna hear her laugh again.*

Every now and then, Midnight thought his dream could come true somehow. He listened when words and whispers and talk blew through the rows: "Jake ran off. The pattyrollers almost catched Sophie, but she's near about North by now. Custus, hear tell, got all the way down to Mexico somehow!"

Midnight would tremble when he heard this news. Could he ever run away? Leave his family

❋

15

behind? What if he got the chance? Would he? He often wondered. *What must it be like to walk that walk of a free man, with no whip at your tail, no chains 'round your feet? Even water must taste sweeter when a body can just stride over and scoop it up without askin' and without waitin'!*

Midnight had heard talk that his mama's mama had been born free in Africa. Talk was that she was a powerful fighting woman, that no overseer could keep her down. She could pick three hundred pounds of cotton on a bad day and chop wood and handle a plow good as any man. People said the day Grandma Fanny finally broke down and cried was also the day she died—when all six of her children were taken away from her in Louisiana and sold away.

Midnight wanted to know about it. He wanted so badly to ask Mama about freedom. About her mama. What part of the stories was true? What was just sweet lies the slaves kept telling, hoping to become strong like Grandma Fanny? But Mama never spoke much about anything after Nile died and Lady got sold. And she surely didn't speak about her family.

✳

16

As Midnight grew older, he couldn't keep Grandma Fanny out of his mind. He was burning to ask. One day when he and his mama were picking side by side he had his chance. The sun was a hot ball up in the sky, and the overseer was across the field on the other side. Midnight dropped his voice low.

"Mama, did Grandma Fanny remember how she feel bein' free?"

The sun flashed off Mama's face as she stood straight up like a rod. Seemed like fire shot out from her eyes. Midnight had never seen that look before.

"Femi!" She hissed at him. "My mama named Femi! She never talk about free. Never. Some things too precious for words, Midnight. Just too precious for plain old words." Then Mama leaned back down. She didn't raise her head again from the ground, just picked cotton faster and faster.

Midnight's heart pounded hard after his mama spoke. He was bothered because he could feel Mama's hurt, but he couldn't understand what she'd meant. *What could be so precious?* He hoped that someday, somehow, he would figure it out.

⸺⸺

Papa snatched time away from the evening hours to be with Midnight. They'd walk through the woods in the moonlight.

"Listen!" Papa would say. "Hear that?" Midnight would strain his young ears. He'd catch a faint scratching sound. Papa would point up a tree, and there would be a possum scrambling along the branch!

That was how Midnight learned to name an

animal from its sounds and smells. On the way back Papa would show him safe wild berries and greens to eat. Sundays they didn't go to the field. Sometimes Papa sat with him and helped him practice tying knots in old pieces of rope. Papa knew all about it because he wrapped and tied the big bales of cotton after it was picked. Sometimes Midnight and Papa would go down to the creek to fish. Papa showed him how to lie on his belly at the edge of the bank and catch a fish with his bare fingers.

Papa taught Midnight that animals could smell fear on a human. He told Midnight to stand tall against any beast, on four legs or two. Midnight was a fast thinker, and he learned his lessons from his father well.

One night, when he was almost thirteen, Papa called Midnight out of a deep sleep. Midnight half-opened and wondered what the fuss was.

"Midnight!" There was Papa's voice again. Midnight squinted and scanned the dark cabin. He didn't see Mama and Papa on their sleeping mat by the door. He rubbed his eyes to see better. His two little sisters, Truth and Queen, were curled together on their sleeping pallet like they should be.

"Come out, son!" Midnight stumbled to the door. He followed the sound of Papa's low whisper around to the back of their shack, to the edge of the piney woods. *What's goin' on? Why is Papa hidin' out here in the dead of night?*

Papa was sitting cross-legged on the ground. He motioned for Midnight to sit beside him. When he spoke his voice didn't get much louder than the whisper. Midnight looked around for Mama, but he couldn't see her anywhere.

"Midnight," Papa said, "you know there's a war goin' on. North fightin' South over slavery."

Midnight shook away the sleep. "Is it over?" he exclaimed. Papa looked him straight in the eyes.

"Hold on, now, son. Nobody won anything yet. But if North wins, we be free. If South wins, I reckon freedom will stay a dream. For me, anyhow."

"Papa . . ." Midnight's mind started racing. *What does he mean? Sounds like Papa's talkin' about runnin' away, but . . .*

"Midnight, be still. This farm is like a hornet's nest. This mornin' master Greely and the overseer up and went to join the fight. Left that son of his and me in charge. Talk is that all the white menfolk around these parts are rushin' off to help the South win the war. Can you beat that? Greely goes off to fight 'cause he says slaves ain't as good as he is, yet he leaves me to help his boy run his farm?"

Midnight couldn't understand any of it.

"Papa, you got my head spinnin'. Just what are you sayin'?"

Papa put a hand on Midnight's shoulder. "Your mama and me been talkin'. We gonna get you outta here."

Papa stepped back in the shadows and led a shining black horse out. Midnight's eyes were wide with wonder and fear.

"Papa . . . this one of the new ridin' horses Master just bought!"

"And he's fast, too! Maybe fast enough to get you far away from here. You take him," Papa said, shoving the reins into Midnight's hands. "He got no marks, yet. No brands. Take him."

Midnight raised a trembling hand to touch the animal. The horse looked straight into his eyes. *If any white folks find out that Papa took this horse for me, he'll be whipped to his death for sure!* Midnight dropped his hand.

"No, Papa. No. I can't let you do this."

"He's called by Dahomey," Papa said, ignoring him. "And he's gonna get my boy to a better life." When Midnight heard Papa say that, he knew: *I might find my dream. I might be free. But I'll be free alone.*

Mama was suddenly standing with them, quiet as still water. Her eyes were sad, but not a tear rolled down her face. Midnight tried to let this moment sink into his mind. Mama touched his cheek with her long rough hand.

"We lost Nile to death. They took Lady away from us. We can't let neither happen to you." Midnight caught her fingers.

"I can't do it, Mama! Much as I wanna be . . . free . . . I can't leave y'all like this!"

Then Mama did something Midnight would never forget. She smiled at him. "We are *always* with you, Midnight Son." She bent over quickly, ripping a piece off the bottom of her faded skirt. She tied the cloth like a bandanna around Midnight's neck.

"Mama—maybe I should wait . . . " Midnight fumbled with the cloth.

"This is the time," Mama said. "Papa can handle young Greely. When we first hear of this war, Papa made this plan. Now go. Be safe. Be strong, my Midnight Son!"

Papa pushed him toward the horse. Then he handed him three things: a small gourd of water hung on a leather cord, a burlap sack the size of a fist, and, last, his own worn felt hat.

"Ride by night." Those were Papa's last words to him.

Midnight took a deep breath and Papa helped him climb onto the horse. "I swear by Grandma Femi, Mama. I'll find freedom. I'll be everything you hope." Seemed like he could feel Mama's arms around him as he rode off into the moonlight, not looking back. He blinked. In his mind he could see Papa's big, dusty brown hands lifting heavy bales of cotton. He blinked again. Saw Queen's round, coffee-brown face and Truth's one-sided smile. He squeezed his eyes hard and a fuzzy picture of Lady formed in his mind. Midnight opened his eyes wide. He couldn't look back. He kept on looking ahead.

So he slapped Dahomey's side and whispered into his big ears, "Yo, yip! Yip! Get on up. Go!" Dahomey stretched his big black head and galloped like the wind.

three

Midnight and Dahomey traveled by moonlight, hiding wherever they could by day. That was easy in this part of Texas, where trees and farmland spread out around them. Midnight hardly slept. Toward the end of each night, just before sunrise, he would start looking for someplace to hide. And he was always on the lookout for the slave catchers called pattyrollers.

Four days into his journey, Midnight had slowed Dahomey to a walk. They were looking east toward daybreak. Midnight still knew the country around him, and he was pretty sure the main road was at least an hour's ride away from the clump of pines he saw ahead. The branches were thick and low to the ground, just right for him and Dahomey to disappear into. As Midnight climbed slowly off

Dahomey, he felt a noise. *Somebody's comin'*, he thought.

Midnight pulled the horse's reins in tight and didn't make another move. A few seconds passed. The feeling he'd had—something like air moving past his head—became a real sound. Just a rustle of grass, but a sound just the same. Midnight was afraid.

He slapped Dahomey's rump and the horse moved slowly off into the bushes, looking back at Midnight like he didn't agree with the decision. Midnight jerked his head around, up, down—looking for someplace to go. Three feet to his left was a shallow ditch, overgrown with some kind of thick weeds. Midnight dropped to the ground with a dull thump. He rolled down and crouched there, listening.

"Aw, Shel, I believe we done got lost now. . . . Ain't no road 'round here!" an older white man's voice drawled.

"Well, seems like somebody's used this trail. Lookahere." A younger voice was close.

Midnight closed his eyes. *Maybe if I can't see them,* he figured, *they can't see me neither.*

"Look!" the old man said. Sweat beaded up on Midnight's nose. "Shel, there's ya trailblazer over yonder. Looks like a runaway horse."

The young voice got closer. "Roy, who'd be fool enough to let an animal this good wander off?"

"There's lots of fools in this world, Shel. We ain't got time to figure it out."

"You mean we ain't got time to make a little money? I didn't see no marks on the horse. If we took him with us, we might sell him for a good price!"

"Mmm." The men moved off in the direction Dahomey had gone. Midnight held his breath. *If they take a mind to grab Dahomey, I'm in for a harder time than I planned for.*

But then the old man seemed to make up his mind. "Shel, we ain't got no time to deal with a stray horse. Ours are stubborn enough. I'm tellin' you, that road must be a good hour's ride north of here. If I don't make it, you'll be the one to pay!" The old man's voice was fading away. The young man was so close Midnight heard his breathing. He made a clucking sound. Midnight didn't move. The sun was fully up now, shining through his closed eyelids. The man started moving away. Midnight slumped against the dirt, relieved.

Midnight stayed right where he was. He held his muscles tight like springs, listening for trouble. A few times tiredness took over and his eyes felt too heavy to keep open. He dreamed about his little sisters holding Mama's skirt and laughing. He dreamed of Lady handing him a warm biscuit that she'd hidden in her apron. That's when he jerked himself awake. Remembering them made his chest start to ache. His head pounded. Right now he didn't want to remember his family so much. So Midnight decided it was best to think about something different.

What if they catch Dahomey? No matter. I'll have to go on by foot. Papa risked his neck gettin' me that horse, though. I can't just forget about it. Besides, I can gain more ground on horseback. I guess I gotta find him.

Midnight raised his head from the ditch and climbed out. The dry earth was covered with horse tracks.

Take it slow and easy. He hunched down close to the ground and followed the tracks with his eyes. At first they seemed hopelessly jumbled. Then he began to see the patterns of the horses. A little distance away the tracks broke into two sets. One group of eight hoof marks went off to the right. Another set, only four, headed straight ahead. Midnight set out behind them.

The sun began to fill the sky, but Midnight kept on following the tracks. He wandered through bushes and tried to keep out of sight near the tall wild grasses sprouting all around. His eyes were on the tracks when he felt someone—or something—looking at him from behind.

"Boy, you make one move and I shoot!" a young man's voice drawled. Midnight froze. His stomach flopped. He knew that voice from the plantation.

"Now you turn around real slow." Midnight did. He stood face to face with Ben Greely, the son of the man who owned the plantation. Young Greely was only seventeen, but he had always acted like a grown man around the slaves. Midnight stared at the gun.

Gotta keep my eyes down, or he'll kill me for sure. He's nothin' but a kid, like me, tryin' to prove that he's a real man. How could I let myself get caught by the likes of him? Midnight lowered his head. His heart pounded hard. Sweat began to roll down his neck.

"Dirty black thief!" Midnight tried to duck away as he heard the ground crunch under Ben's feet, but he didn't move fast enough.

WHUMP! The butt of the rifle rammed the side of Midnight's head, knocking him sprawling in the dust. Midnight passed out.

He woke up in darkness. His head and eyes ached. His body was twisted, his wrists tied behind his back. His arms and legs were bound. He was lying on his side with his knees pressed up against his face. It was hot, hard to breathe. He blinked and tried to move. His shoulders hit something hard. Wood. Then he tried to stretch his feet. Wood.

I'm in a box! Midnight wanted to shout out, but he clenched his mouth shut. He tried to relax his body and listen to the sounds outside.

"Come on. We've gotta find that horse!" Ben Greely was close, almost on top of the box.

"Now, Mr. Ben. We can't go draggin' this box all over creation! Let's just take him back and forget about the animal."

Midnight knew that voice, too. It was Dan, another one of the field slaves. Dan was about the same age as Midnight's papa. He'd worked many hours alongside Papa, picking cotton. *Ben won't like nothin' a slave has to say,* Midnight thought.

"That's funny, Dan." Ben snorted. "I mean, you talkin' about the horse like you ain't a stupid beast, too! Now, I'm gonna get all my father's property back, and you're gonna help me!" Dan fell silent.

Who's stupid? He ain't even figured out that my papa gave me the horse. He thinks I stole it on my own! Ben kept talking. "We'll just leave him here in the box. The horse can't be too far off." Midnight shifted his weight. He was able to turn his head a little. A tiny line of light fell across his face. There was a crack between the planks on the top of the box.

Midnight jerked his body angrily against the wood. *I gotta get out of here!*

"You ain't goin' nowhere!" Ben growled, almost as if he'd heard Midnight's thinking. He kicked the box, making Midnight's head slam against the inside. Midnight closed his eyes. His mind wandered back many years . . .

—•—

It was before they'd been sold. Midnight had learned to toddle around the baby cabin. One day his sister Lady came from the kitchen with some bread scraps. This time, she came with the slave owner's wife. Midnight sat on the floor and watched them walk around, throwing meat bones and hunks of stale bread to the babies. When they started to leave, Midnight scrambled to his feet and followed them to the door.

"What's this?" The mistress swirled her big skirt around and looked down at Midnight. He stopped, keeping his eyes on her.

"Midnight!" Lady hissed. "Go on back!" Her eyes widened with fear. She tried to pull him away, but she was small and he was strong.

"Just where does he think he's goin'?" the woman asked. She wasn't speaking to Midnight, but to Lady.

"OUT!" Midnight shouted, stomping his foot.

✳

The woman raised her eyebrows. "Oh!" She laughed in a surprised way. "You want to go out, do you?" She leaned down to look at him. He stared at her.

"Go out." Midnight repeated what the woman had said. She laughed.

"Well, I declare! This little black thing can talk and all! Lady, let him come on out. If he can do all this talkin', we'll find him something useful to do." She stood up and turned on her heel, walking toward the big house. Midnight followed right behind. He never did go back inside the shack. He had gotten out.

Midnight's eyes flew open. Now there was no light coming through the crack in the box top. The only sound was an owl hooting far off in the distance. He jerked his body like he had before and waited for the boot—or something else. Nothing happened.

They're gone. This is my chance. Midnight curled his fingers up to the rope around his wrists. He could touch the knotted part of the rope. Papa's words came to him.

"If you can tie a good-holding knot, Midnight, you can *loose* a good-holding knot." Midnight took a deep breath and worked his fingers at the rope. It didn't take long. He smiled to himself as the rope dropped from his hands.

Ha! Papa always said Dan couldn't tie his own boot strings, if he ever got any. It was harder to arch his back and twist his body in the box to get at the ankle rope, but he did. Now he could move a little more. He squirmed and rolled his shoulders until his body was upside down. His feet were flat against the top of the box.

WHAM! Midnight slammed his feet onto the wood. It didn't move. Again, and again. Still the top wouldn't move.

Seems like Dan is a lot better at building boxes than tyin' rope. Midnight hit it over and over until his knees burned. The bottoms of his feet were numb. *THUMP! WHAM!* He could see a slice of night sky. *Now I'm gettin' it.* He turned his body so that he could push with his arms. The nails were screeching out of the wood all around, but he couldn't push the top off. *I ain't got time for this.* He twisted back to the first position.

He thought of Ben Greely ramming the rifle butt on his head. He pictured the boy's face in front of him, grinning. Then he pressed his back into the bottom of the box, drew in his knees, and let his feet go.

WHAM! The wood pieces flew up into the night.

✳

Midnight tried to jump up, but his muscles and joints felt like they were on fire. He stood up slowly and stepped out of the box, quickly crouching to the ground. The top had come off in two clean pieces. He picked them up. A nail hung out of one end, and he found another on the ground. He looked around and spotted a big, smooth rock. In a few minutes, he'd put the top back on the box.

That won't fool 'em long, but it'll give me some time. Midnight saw his hat and sack crumpled in the brush. He gathered them up and looked for horse tracks. Then he set out through the bushes.

He trailed Dan and Ben by moonlight for miles until he saw a flickering light in the distance. He dropped to his knees and crawled closer.

Dan was sitting with the rifle across his knees. The foolish boy was hunkered down under a blanket, asleep. And there was Dahomey, tied between their two horses a few feet away. Midnight blinked. Dan turned his head. They were staring right at each other!

If I lose my nerve now, I'm dead. I guess I don't have no choice. With his eyes on Dan all the time, Midnight slowly circled the little camp, stopping at the horses. He hadn't made a sound. Ben's horse shifted his weight, and Ben rolled over in his sleep. Dan kept looking at Midnight. Almost without moving, he tilted his head in a nod. Then he turned away. Still watching Dan, Midnight crawled under Ben's horse to the tethering rope staked into the ground. As quickly as he could make his fingers fly, Midnight had set all three horses free. He calmly backed Dahomey away from the others. Back, back . . . Ben didn't stir, and Dan didn't look again. Midnight grabbed the reins up and slung himself across Dahomey's back, squeezing his knees into the horse's flanks. Dahomey broke into a trot, then a run.

"You son of a gun!" Midnight whispered. "I got you back!" How long it was before Ben Greely discovered the horse was gone, he never knew. Midnight felt bad that Dan had been part of his getaway. He only hoped that Ben wasn't smart enough to figure out how Dan had helped.

four

Pretty soon they'd been on the run over a week. Midnight tried to keep up with time by making notches on a stick with an old arrow flint he'd found. One notch for each sundown.

He began to relax, but didn't know why. Maybe it was because tricking Ben Greely had made him feel strong. Real strong. And, so far, there was no sign of another soul. Even though the Texas territory was awfully big, there were two other plantations near abouts. Yet Greely had had to come out with just Dan. No search party. Something had surely happened to all the other white men. *They must be goin' off in droves to fight. Maybe this war is bigger and badder than folks thought it was gonna be.*

Midnight was hunched up in a tall oak tree when the sun set. *Twelve days,* he counted on his stick. He glanced down at Dahomey. The horse was hidden yards away, in a little valley behind some scrub bushes. Midnight had figured it was best to put Dahomey as far away as he could, still keeping him in sight. Dahomey had become a good partner, learning to sense Midnight's moods and understand the boy's movements. He seemed to know the danger they were up against.

Midnight opened the burlap sack Papa had given him. There were two hunks of salted pork and one small, hard bit of stale corn bread left. He decided he'd better save the meat. So he shoved the corn bread in his mouth and shut his eyes tight as he rolled it around his cheeks, pretending that it was Mama's hot hoecake. He told himself and his belly that it was enough to make him feel full. The hours passed.

When I'm free, Midnight thought, *my belly will always be full.* His old daydreams came back. He imagined far-off places. He saw himself striding out across open spaces, no cotton anywhere around. *Aw, I can feel the money janglin' in my pocket!*

For the first time, Midnight wondered how. How could he do all that? He shaded his eyes with his hand and looked off in the direction of the setting sun. West. Then he turned and looked the other way. *Where am I gonna go? No point in tryin' to make it up*

✳

North. I'd hafta go back through Texas, Louisiana. . . . A black boy, travelin' alone, tryin' to cut through a war? Naw, naw. Pattyrollers would catch me for sure.

Midnight looked back in the direction of that rosy, lazy sun. It was something to look at!

"Sakes alive!" he mumbled aloud, leaning back against the tree trunk. "I ain't never seen nothin' look that good. That old sun's like a big pink egg or somethin'!" Midnight knew right then how he wanted to spend his free life: riding and roaming under that sun. He had to go west.

Seemed like Mexico was the way to go, since he'd heard that there wasn't any slavery there. Maybe out in Mexico he could find work on a farm or even a ranch. Maybe he could become a cowpoke. *'Course, I'd have lots to learn. But I know it would be worth it. Then I could stay out and about day and night, gettin' paid to be free.*

Midnight scrambled down from the tree as dusk came. He eased onto Dahomey and headed for that red ball in the sky. The setting sun led Midnight across the Texas prairie like a banner that only he could see.

Dahomey galloped on, night after night. That horse knew just which way to go. Luck was riding with them. When the corn bread was long gone, Midnight gnawed on his pork and found wild

✳
36

berries and dandelion greens. He'd had a chance to fill his water gourd at some streams he'd passed. One cloudy night, weeks after they'd started, Midnight was startled by a big, spiny lizard darting across some nearby rocks. He was tired, and mistook the lizard for a snake. He dropped his counting stick and couldn't find it on the ground. So he and Dahomey kept on without it.

After a few more days, it became harder and harder for Midnight to find any berries or plants that looked familiar. He was afraid to eat anything he hadn't seen before. The water stayed low. Midnight began to lose count of how long he'd been riding and hiding.

The look of the land around him started changing. There were fewer and fewer trees. Tall, spiny cactuses dotted the dusty ground. The occasional ponds they came across were small and shallow. There were hills far off, and Midnight spied fewer clumps of low green bushes spread over the rugged ground. This was a different part of Texas.

When the nights ended and daylight came again, all Midnight could do was slide off Dahomey and ease his shaky legs to the ground, lying beside the nearest bunch of thorny-looking bushes. His friend Sun now started feeling awfully strong on Midnight's head and shoulders. Even with his hat shading them, his eyes danced around like they belonged in someone else's head. There was no more bread, no more meat. No creeks or streams in sight, either.

One night Midnight's whole body throbbed from hunger and plain tiredness. His mouth and throat were dry. Somehow he pulled himself up onto Dahomey's back. Midnight's thoughts were all scrambled now. He missed his mama and papa something terrible, but he couldn't remember where they were. A wave of fear passed through his body. He was afraid he was losing his senses.

Where am I goin'? He couldn't even remember. Dahomey was tired, too; still, he trotted faithfully through the night with Midnight barely hanging on. With his head pressed to Dahomey's warm back, Midnight began to think he could hear things. Not just night animals, not just his own whistling breaths. He really believed that he could hear people.

"*Mira, mira!*"

"*Que pasa?*"

"*Ay! Es un hijo Negrito!*"

Midnight couldn't understand the voices. He tried opening his eyes to see who was talking, but he couldn't. He slid off Dahomey's back, not to the hard ground, but into someone's strong arms.

Midnight opened his eyes slowly. His body still ached. His head was on fire. He was inside a cool, dark room. Fear grabbed his stomach and it hurt. *Have I been caught? Where am I? Where is Dahomey?* Midnight threw back the striped blanket that covered his legs and sat up fast. He felt so light-headed that he swayed back, catching hold of the edge of the wooden cot. His elbow hit a table beside the bed. A shiny tin cup tinkled to the floor.

"Ah!" A woman stepped into the room. Midnight stiffened. Was this who caught him? Would she turn him in? The woman smiled and stepped toward him. She was brown but not as dark as Midnight. A shining red-brown. She walked boldly, with her hands on her hips and lots of straight black hair swinging when she moved. She walked like a great big woman, but she was the tiniest grown woman Midnight had ever seen.

"You, free." Silver bracelets bounced and jangled on the woman's arms as she pointed at Midnight.

"Free?" Midnight repeated the word. He still didn't move. A man's voice called from another room.

"Hola!"

"Venga!" the woman answered. "Juan Diego, *venga a ver!"* Midnight realized they were talking some other language.

✳

"W-Where am I?" he asked, his heart beating fast.

A short, square-built man with bowed legs stood in the doorway. He smiled at Midnight. His face was wrinkled all over.

"Well, *bueno!* You do not know where you are?"

"Naww, sir . . ." Midnight said slowly.

"My friend, you are in Mexico. I am Juan Diego Sanchez Rivera."

Midnight blew out a deep breath. "Mexico? I made it!" His words ran out. "The lady said—I'm free? Am I? I—" He suddenly felt light-headed again. The lady was by him all at once, holding a cup of something hot. It smelled like chicken. He sipped. Whatever it was, it was good. Midnight drank a little, then the lady eased him back down onto the bed. Juan Diego patted Midnight's shoulder.

"*Sí,* yes. You are free. No more a slave."

"So—that talkin' I heard was Mexican?"

"Spanish. It is the language we speak here."

"My horse—" Midnight went on.

"Rest. Rest now." Juan Diego stopped him. "What is your name, my young friend?"

Midnight didn't answer right away. Most slave owners let slave parents pick a first name for their children. But the last name was always the owner's last name. Always. Midnight made up his mind. *I ain't owned no more.*

"My name's Midnight. Midnight Son."

Juan Diego nodded. "Ah. In my language, your name is *Medianoche*. Midnight. I am pleased to meet you, Mr. Son." He turned to the woman. "*Se llama* Midnight Son. *Medianoche.*" Then he said to Midnight, "This is my sister, Milagros. She will take good care of you."

Midnight tried to wrap his tongue around her name. "*Mee—la—*"

Juan Diego smiled. "*Mee-la-grrr-oss*. To you it means *miracles.*"

Midnight looked at her. "Thank you, Miss Miracles."

"That's *gracias*, 'thank you,' " Juan Diego told him. "I am the only one around here who can speak your language. We could tell when we found you that . . ." He stopped, searching for the right thing to say, ". . . that you were trying to escape from something. Here in Mexico, slavery is against the law. Milagros made me teach her how to say *free* so she could be the first to tell you."

"*Gracias*," Midnight said again. Miss Miracles put her hand to her lips and motioned for him to be quiet. Midnight was tired anyway. There was so much to think about! *I'm free! I'm in*

Mexico! I got people lookin' out for me. People who seem to care.

"*Ya*, Juan Diego. *De'jele descansar.*" Miss Miracles shooed the man away. Juan Diego waved his hat. "Until tomorrow, Midnight Son. We will speak of your future tomorrow." Miss Miracles pulled Midnight's blanket up and left. Midnight looked at the ceiling. *This sure is a miracle,* he thought. *Some kind of miracle has happened to me.*

Juan Diego did come the next day, and the next. Miss Miracles wouldn't even let Midnight get out of bed. On the third day, he was still a little shaky on his feet, but when Juan Diego came, Midnight walked out of the house with him. The first thing they did was find Dahomey. The horse was in a small fenced yard behind Miss Miracles' house, brushed, watered, and fed. Midnight was satisfied with that.

They went back around front, past Miss Miracles' chickens. Midnight looked at the house up close. It looked like a big square rock—as dusty and wind-smooth as the hills around it. But Miss Miracles had a patch of green garden right in front of the house, with big red flowers climbing up a wooden frame around her doorway.

Scattered around were other little houses like hers. Most didn't look so neat and quiet, but even the smallest ones were bigger and sturdier than the shacks back home. Goats and chickens and dogs ran everywhere. Along the road ahead, Midnight saw a few trees and some sheds and barns. Past that he could see the road winding away between some hills. A few little children chased each other around the houses. They made Midnight think of his own little sisters, but he pushed that out of his mind.

"This, Midnight Son, is the village," Juan Diego was telling him. "The road leads out to Hacienda de la Suerte. You could call it Ranch of Luck."

Midnight stopped walking. "Ranch!" he almost shouted. "Mr. Juan Diego—you think I could get work?"

Juan Diego let out a laugh. "You want to be a *vaquero*? A cowboy? What do you know about it?"

"Not much," Midnight admitted. "I took care of cows, that's all."

"So, you are ready to learn, Midnight Son?" Juan Diego looked hard into Midnight's eyes. "Maybe you are too young to be a *vaquero*."

"Juan Diego, I already spent my whole life workin' like a demon for somebody who didn't pay me nothin'. You bet I'm ready to work for somethin' of my own!"

"Then, my friend—*amigo*—I am the one to help you."

"You?"

Juan Diego laughed. "Why, yes. I am the fore-man on Hacienda de la Suerte!"

Midnight couldn't believe it. "I need work," he said.

Juan Diego rubbed his chin. "Can you ride today?"

"I could ride now—" Midnight began. But Juan Diego put a hand on the boy's shoulder and shook his head.

"Not now. I will come for you after the midday meal, yes?"

"Yes, yes, sir!" Midnight smiled. It had been a long time since he'd done that. Juan Diego walked away, waving. "Until then—*hasta luego!*"

Midnight leaned back against Miss Miracles' fence post and looked out at the low red hills. He was beginning to feel different inside. For years he'd had a hard hurting place in his chest. Whenever he thought about Nile, or how his mama had changed, it felt like something heavy was lying on top of him. After a while the feeling never left him. It was always there. Today, somehow, it didn't feel so heavy. He remembered back to that time in the field when he'd tried to get Mama to talk about his grandma.

"Some things too precious for words," Mama had said. Midnight smiled a little to himself. *This bein' free—bein' in charge of my own self—is somethin' special for*

44

sure. I can't explain the way I feel now to nobody. I feel good, plain good. Sort of calm and peaceful inside, but there's somethin' more. No words seem right to explain it. Wonder if that was what Mama meant? There ain't no words right enough to explain feelin' free.

Midnight looked up at the sun. Noon was hours away. His body still ached a bit, but his head was clear and he wanted to do something. *Maybe I can help Miss Miracles,* he thought, turning back to the house.

"Hello? Miss Miracles? Hello?" The house had only two rooms—the small one Midnight had woken up in and a bigger one with a fireplace. No one was inside. Midnight went back out. "Anybody about?"

"*Hola!*" a woman's voice called out from behind the house. Midnight found Miss Miracles standing near an outdoor oven. It looked like a big clay beehive with a chimney sticking out of the top. *Just like on the plantation—when it's hotter than the devil inside, they take all the cooking outside so the house stays cool.* Miss Miracles stirred the big iron pot hanging from a heavy iron hook over the fire. The wonderful smell of bubbling beans floated up. Steam curled around Miss Miracles' head. She looked up at Midnight and smiled.

Miss Miracles stepped over to a long plank table near the oven. She dipped her hand into a small iron

✳

45

pot and scooped out a handful of white corn kernels. They seemed soft. She dropped the wet corn onto a kind of stone tray and picked up what looked like a stone rolling pin. *Lady used to use one of those things when she worked in the kitchen.*

Midnight sat on the ground and watched. She sprinkled some water over the corn, then began to rub the stone over it. Her movements were fast and smooth. Back and forth, over and over. The corn slowly turned into a mound of soft dough. She took the dough off the tray and worked the mound with her hands, kneading and squeezing it. Then she pinched off a bit of dough, slapping and patting it until it began to get flatter.

Slap! Slap! The dough was like a flat, round cake. *Slap! Slap!* The cake became thinner and thinner. She had made a big, thin circle. She put it onto a big iron griddle and slid the griddle into the oven. Finally, she scooped out more dough and started all over again. Midnight wondered what she was making.

Midnight closed his eyes and listened to the gentle slapping and patting sounds. They were almost like a song. He leaned against the wall of the house, hearing the animals and the laughing children far away. Soon he was sleeping.

five

"Eat! Eat!" Midnight jerked awake, blinking. Then he focused his eyes on the corral across the backyard, where Dahomey was looking back at him. Miss Miracles peeped around the house, beckoning with her arm full of bangles. "Eat!" she called.

"Yes, ma'am!" Midnight scrambled up, seeing that the sun was high in the sky. Juan Diego would be coming soon. He went back inside.

Miss Miracles had baked the flat cakes and stacked them inside a cloth to keep them warm. She removed the cloth and Midnight looked at the cakes, then at her.

"*Es tortilla,*" she said slowly. "*Tor-tee-ah! Mira!*" She picked up one of the cakes, spooned some cooked beans and vegetables into the middle, rolled it up, and bit off one end.

✳

47

Midnight smiled and nodded. He did the same. "Mmmm. Good," he mumbled.

"*Tortilla,*" Miss Miracles said again.

"*Tor-tee-ah,*" Midnight repeated. He realized that he was learning the Spanish language.

"Midnight Son!" Juan Diego looked into the house and swung his wide-brimmed hat off his head. "Let's go."

Midnight gulped his coffee and stuffed the last of the tortilla into his mouth. "Thank you, Miss Miracles," he breathed, rushing out. He pulled on his own hat as he headed for the corral. Dahomey saw him coming and trotted right toward him. Midnight opened the gate and led the horse out. He checked his animal's bridle and bit, looked all around his legs and hooves. Then he eased his sore body onto Dahomey's back.

"You ride with no saddle?" Juan Diego asked, heading his black mustang for the road.

"Never had use for one," Midnight answered. "Back home, I was in the cotton field. This here's the only horse I really had to ride."

Juan Diego laughed. "And ride him you did . . . all the way to Mexico!" They broke the horses into a fast gallop. A warm wind blew against Midnight's ears. He leaned into Dahomey's neck. *Boy, you smell wild and, well, free. You sure don't smell like a stable, or like leather from a saddle.*

A low wooden fence edged the road on the left. The trees were standing in orderly-looking rows on the other side. Midnight saw a few grazing cows in the distance beyond the fence. Ahead on the left was a huge gate—it seemed to be made of small tree trunks lashed tightly together. Above the gate was a hanging sign with words painted on it. Beside the words was a picture of a horseshoe with a wiggly line through it.

Midnight looked away from the sign. He couldn't read it. No one in his family could. Slaves on the Greely plantation weren't even allowed to touch books. The punishment for man, woman, or child was thirty lashes with the bullwhip. Nobody he knew had ever found the backbone—or the chance—to go against it. He sure hadn't.

Juan Diego said, "Here is Hacienda de la Suerte, Midnight Son. Perhaps your luck is here, also." They slowed the horses to a walk and passed through the gate.

Midnight opened his eyes wide. His heart began to beat harder and faster. This was the ranch. A low wooden house even bigger than the Big House on the plantation spread out to the right. It had a funny-looking, flat red roof shining out from behind some trees.

"What's that roof made with?" he asked, trying to take a closer look.

✼

Juan Diego answered without turning around. "It is clay, baked into curved shapes. . . . In your words it is called *tile*, I think."

A noisy bunch of voices behind the house somewhere caught Midnight's attention. Juan Diego rode in that direction. Midnight followed.

Four or five men were shouting near a big corral. Inside, a man was slowly walking toward a brown horse on the other side of the yard. The man raised his hand and the other men fell quiet. Midnight could see that the man held a bridle in one hand. As he got closer to the horse, it took a few steps back. The man kept going closer. Then, in one quick movement, he slipped the bit into the horse's mouth, whispered to the animal, and slipped the headstall over his ears. The horse shook his head violently, but the man held on. He reached down and grabbed a saddle, slinging it up onto the animal's back. The horse moved impatiently as the man strapped the saddle on. Then he swung up onto the horse. That was it.

Dust clouds flew everywhere. The biggest was inside the corral. Suddenly the bucking brown horse and rider leaped out of the cloud with the horse snorting and neighing like mad. The rider hung on with both hands, slipping and sliding but staying on. Midnight had never seen anything like it. He stopped Dahomey and hopped off.

The brown horse was angry but now seemed to

be fighting with only half his strength. The man hung on.

"You got him now, pardner!" one of the men shouted. Midnight was surprised to hear somebody speaking a language he understood.

"*Arriba! Arriba!*"

"*Sí,* Estebaño!"

By now the horse wasn't kicking so high or snorting. The man leaned in to the horse's ears. In a little while, the horse slowed to a walk. The rider looked up at the others, smiling. He was in control. He turned the horse away and trotted him around the yard.

"That is Estebaño. He is what you call a bronco-buster. The best we have here." Juan Diego had walked up beside Midnight. "Tie your horse and come to meet the others." Three of the men were Mexican, but the one who had spoken American had yellow, straw-colored hair and bright blue eyes. He looked evenly at Midnight and stuck out his rough, sun-browned hand.

"Howdy. I'm Riley. Jim Riley."

Midnight stared at the man's hand. No white man had ever spoken to him that way. Man-to-man, that is. For sure, no white man had ever tried to shake his hand! The man didn't seem to notice Midnight's surprise. Slowly, Midnight raised his right hand.

"I am Midnight Son." He stretched his fingers toward Riley's. Riley grabbed Midnight's hand with a firm grip, shook hard, and nodded.

"I see you're used to hard work. You'll be welcome around here, Midnight." Juan Diego introduced Midnight to the others, but Midnight barely heard. He was still amazed over the handshake.

"With this new bunch of mustangs to break in, we could use somebody to help out," Riley was saying to Juan Diego.

"Just what I was thinking," Juan Diego agreed. "My friend Midnight can use the work, *sí*?" Midnight nodded. "Then I will talk to the boss right now."

He strode away toward the house. That left Midnight in the middle of the other men. The Mexican fellows looked at him and walked off to the stables. Riley stayed. Midnight felt so uncomfortable that he didn't say anything. Riley finally broke the silence. He wasn't looking at Midnight; he kept his eyes fixed on some longhorns way off in the distance.

"Look, fella, I heard how Milagros found you and I can guess your story. But these Mexicans will be good to you, believe me."

Midnight's eyes narrowed a bit. He hadn't really thought about it, but this town must be a small place. *Everybody must know how I rode up all raggedy and dirty in the night and fell off my horse. What if there's a bounty on my head and somebody 'round here wants the money?* Riley was still talking.

"They'll do anything to kick the gringos—that's what they call white folks—in the teeth. See, it hasn't been that long since the good old United States took Texas away from Mexico, and the Mexican people haven't forgot it."

Midnight was surprised to find out that Texas could have belonged to some foreign country. But it was easy to understand how Mexican folks might still be mad about it. *Kinda like your neighbor stealin' your shirt, then wearin' it right in your face.* Midnight relaxed a little but said nothing yet.

Riley went on. "I don't go along with holding an innocent soul against his will. That's how come I ain't in Texas no more. So if you get on here, and do the job, I'll back you up the same as I would anybody else."

"It don't matter to you, black, white, red, or brown, huh? You sure about that?" Midnight's throat felt tight as he spoke to Riley.

"Sure as that sun's gonna come up tomorrow, pardner!" Riley walked away quickly without turning around. As he went, Juan Diego stepped out on the porch the house, waving his hat.

"It is done! You begin helping with the horses tomorrow. The pay is very small at first, until you learn the horses. But you will get room and board. You can sleep in the bunkhouse here."

"Here? You sleep here too?" Midnight questioned.

"*Sí*, my friend. And tomorrow you will see what I do around here."

"You a broncobuster?" Midnight asked.

"No . . . I herd the cattle. And I use *una reata*." Juan Diego reached toward his saddle and grabbed a coiled-up lariat. It was as thick around as a finger, made of leather strips braided like a little girl's hair. Before Midnight could blink an eye, Juan Diego had snapped his arm out. *CRACK!* The lariat snapped out straight. Juan Diego stepped and moved his wrist, somehow making the lariat roll up into a giant circle.

"Go on, walk through it." Juan Diego laughed. As Midnight stepped into the circle, it fell around him, tightening around his ankles. He tripped, and Juan Diego reached out a hand to keep him from hitting the dust.

"Sakes alive!" Midnight gasped. "I never saw anything like that in my life. So fast!"

"One must be quick, Midnight, to get the cow before it runs away."

"You mean you use that thing to catch cows?" Midnight had run across many a field chasing after stray cows. If only he'd had this rope thing back then.

"When you learn to use *la reata*—the lariat—you

can catch anything." Juan Diego was coiling the lariat again.

Midnight straightened up his shoulders. "Would you show me?"

"If you want it, yes."

"I want it, Mr. Juan Diego!"

Juan Diego handed Midnight the lariat. Midnight touched it with careful fingers. It was firm but felt good in his hand. For a minute, Juan Diego didn't let go of the lariat. He looked Midnight right in his eyes. The smiling face that Midnight was already used to seeing turned serious. Midnight tensed up.

"First, Midnight Son, I am Juan Diego. Only Juan Diego. I am not, and no one will ever again be, your master." Juan Diego went on. "You have a family?" Midnight nodded.

"Then your escape is even more courageous. I can see that when you want a thing, you make it happen. I want you to know that the life of a *vaquero* is not easy."

Midnight found his voice. "I'm not looking for easy, Juan Diego," he said. "I'm looking for the chance to tell my own feet where to go."

Juan Diego let go of the lariat and patted Midnight on the shoulder.

Midnight's whole face smiled. *"Va-kerr-ro. Vaquero,"* he said. "Yeah, that means *cowboy*."

six

Midnight rode Dahomey back to Miss Miracles' to collect his things for the move. He sat on the cot in the little room and spread his kerchief out. As he touched it, he could feel Mama's fingers again, tying it around his neck.

Midnight let himself see all their faces in his mind. Papa's wise eyes. Mama's wide smile and the gap between her front teeth. Truth's round little mouth and Queen's dimpled cheeks. *I miss them somethin' terrible!* Midnight grabbed onto the edges of the cot and shivered so hard that his whole body shook. The cot shook. He could feel a sob bubbling up in his throat, but he swallowed it down and held on till his knuckles hurt. There was nothing he could do to stop it. The shaking lasted a few minutes.

How am I gonna do this? How can I get along by myself?
He could hear Miss Miracles in the other room.
"Gotta pull myself together," he said out loud. He
took a deep breath. Then he was still. He closed his
eyes and gathered his family up and put them back,
far back, in his memory. He had to. There was no
way he could allow this to happen on that ranch.
Not in front of people.

Midnight was calm now. He carefully folded his
old clothes inside the large piece of cloth and pulled
up the corners to knot them.

"Miss Miracles." He walked into the other room.
His empty water gourd was strung from one hand
and he clutched the tied bundle in the other.

Miss Miracles spun her tiny body around from
the fireplace.

"*Sí,* Medianoche." She smiled as she said his
name slowly.

"I-I wanna thank you. Thank you for savin'
my life." He stopped, then remembered. *"Muchas
gr-gracias,"* he added.

Miss Miracles looked from Midnight's face to his
hands. Her smile turned sad. She understood that
Midnight was about to leave.

"*Vaya con Dios,* Medianoche." Before Midnight
could move to the door, she grabbed him and
hugged him tight. "Free!" she whispered, letting

✳

him go. Midnight stepped outside and turned to wave. Miss Miracles stood in her doorway, waving back.

"Dahomey." He rubbed the horse's neck. "Let's get goin'." On his own, Dahomey broke into a fast trot and they were off, leaving a trail of dusty smoke behind.

At the ranch Midnight's new life really began. On the first morning, he got his first pair of boots—he'd never worn shoes before. Juan Diego let Midnight try on his old pair. Midnight pulled them on. He kept looking at his feet. Felt like his toes were trapped inside that smooth, tight brown leather. He tiptoed around. After a few hours he could walk on his flat feet. And in a few days he'd forgotten about the boots except when he glanced down at his feet. There was so much more to pay attention to.

Time flew by. Midnight started every day by feeding all the fine horses kept in the barn and brushing them down. Then he watered and fed the newly broken-in mustangs. Some days Estebaño, the broncobuster, kept him at the corral. Without speaking, he showed Midnight how to deal with the wild horses. Baño never yelled, never whipped them. He always moved slowly and easily, and he talked to the horses. Midnight liked Baño's way.

Every few days Midnight rode out with Juan Diego or Riley to a different section of the huge ranch.

"Now, when you rope a steer, what you want is to bring him down, not choke him to death," Riley told him out on the range. "Make sure you got ease in your rope." He showed Midnight how to loop the rope and knot it loosely so that the knot could slide back and forth.

"Toss it!" Riley commanded. Midnight flung his right arm out and sent the rope spinning, but it never made it over the makeshift steer they had made of rotting fence posts. Midnight practiced over and over.

"I think he needs a moving target," Juan Diego said from his horse. "Mount up, Midnight." Midnight hurried onto Dahomey and followed Juan Diego way out into the pasture. They slowed their horses yards away from two cows calmly chewing grass.

"How do I start?" Midnight asked, eyeing the animals.

"Double back and gallop up from the side. Throw your arm out, like this—" Juan Diego motioned. "As soon as the loop falls over the head, pull back. You must do it quickly, or the sly ones will slip out and away."

Midnight turned Dahomey. He fidgeted with his lariat, knotting and re-knotting it. Finally, he got one that slipped and slid without coming undone.

"All right, boy. We gonna do this thing." Midnight dug his heels into Dahomey's sides and galloped. The cows bolted as soon as they heard Dahomey coming. Midnight chose to follow the larger, tan one. He waited, chasing the cow for five minutes. Then in one movement he threw out the loop and pulled as hard as he could without yanking. The cow jerked her head to the right and out of the loop's way. She stumbled, but, as if she knew what was going on, she trampled the lariat with her hind hooves before she ran off.

Midnight slumped his shoulders. *Seems like I oughta be able to throw a rope better than this! Well, I gotta work on it. I never give up on my first try at nothin'.* He looked over at Juan Diego.

"Do not worry," he said. "All things will come with time. We will try again with another animal. *Vaya!*" He galloped away toward the rest of the herd. Riley yelled, "Get the lariat and come on!" Midnight did as he was told.

For two weeks, Midnight spent his mornings on the range, practicing with the lariat. After supper he rode Dahomey out to the old fence posts, but he knew Juan Diego was right. He needed a moving target. Sunday morning came, and the other cow-pokes started their day off by sleeping in. Midnight hurried out as soon as he heard the old rooster crowing to announce the sunrise. He took Dahomey quietly out of the corral and mounted up.

He rode for an hour before he spotted a group of five cows calmly grazing on sweet grass. For a few minutes, Midnight just sat on Dahomey and watched the other animals. *Before I leave this range today, I'm gonna rope me a cow.* He breathed deeply, fingering his lariat. He'd braided it himself from thin leather strips, just like Juan Diego had shown him. *Here goes.*

Midnight broke Dahomey into a gallop, straight at the cows. They scattered. He chose a brown-and-white-spotted one, turning Dahomey to follow it. The cow was uncommonly fast. Midnight kept up the chase. He snatched up his lariat. In a minute, he had snapped it out in the cow's direction. The rope plopped over the animal's horns, then ears. Midnight nodded, pulling the lariat gently. The cow's head leaned to the left, and she lost her balance. She was down!

Midnight jumped off Dahomey and rushed to the struggling cow, releasing her from the rope before she could get to her feet and drag it away. He felt good. He was learning to be proud.

Midnight didn't have much time to feel lonely at the ranch. He worked long, hard days learning about different ranching jobs. The Mexican cowboys kept to themselves, and he didn't feel comfortable spending too much time with Riley. When he had a spare minute he'd sit under a tree and look toward the western hills. He liked the way the land and the sky seemed to melt together.

One evening Midnight finished his chores early. Sunset was painting soft colors across the hills. Some of the men were still out looking for stray cows. Some were showing off their roping tricks near the corral. The big boss had ridden one of his Andalusians to another ranch to do business. The strong smell of roasting meat told Midnight that the evening mealtime was near.

Midnight went to sit under his favorite tree. It was old, so its trunk was very wide. If Midnight sat in silence no one could see him or know that he was there. He liked that. He settled his back against the tree. This was Midnight's time.

Been here six months, Midnight counted to himself. He stretched out his arms and looked at how much bigger they were getting. *I bet I could throw a powerful distance.* He glanced down at a smooth oval stone about the same size as the palm of his hand. He scooped it up and narrowed his eyes for a target. "Ah," he breathed, sighting a rusty old horseshoe perched on a stump. He sat up straight and closed one eye to aim. Just as he drew back his arm, he heard the noise.

"Ssssss . . . !" Midnight froze. Without turning his head, he moved his eyes hard to the right.

The snake was less than four feet away, reared up to strike. It was a thick brown rattler.

CRAAACK! A bullet whizzed past Midnight's face so close he could feel its breeze. The snake dropped like an old rope into a heap on the ground.

Midnight jerked his head around.

"Better be more careful, kid!" The man was old. His neatly trimmed beard and mustache were silvery gray, just like the bushy brows that shaded his dark eyes. He was big. Well over six feet, chest as round and wide as a barrel. He was well-dressed, too. A bright red calico shirt showed under a vest made of some kind of animal hide, shiny black boots with silver spurs slung around the ankles. Most amazing to Midnight was this: His skin was brown. *He's not brown like Mexican folks, he's brown like me.*

"Uh—thank you—I—" Midnight sputtered.

"Never seen another black cowpoke, huh? Thought you were the only one around? Well,

✳

where've you been?" The man laughed and his whole body shook. He reached to grab Midnight's free hand in both of his.

"Believe it or not, they call me Slim. Mississippi Slim. I'm an old buddy of Juan Diego. He around?" Midnight shook his head.

"Fact is, I'm passing through. Heading back to the Crazy Eight outfit in west Texas. Gonna join a big roundup, then herd 'em on up to Kansas."

Midnight scrambled up from the ground.

"You saved my life. I reckon I owe you." He dropped the rock and looked hard at the dead snake.

"That's how it goes in the West, kid. Gotta be rough and ready. I save your life, you owe me. You save my life—"

"Then we're even!" Midnight finished the sentence. Slim smiled.

"Can I call you Slim?"

"Everybody does. Say, what's your name?"

"Midnight. Midnight Son."

"I like that. A name to be remembered. Midnight Son."

Midnight kept staring. Slim made him think of all the people he'd left behind. The people he'd put away in the back of his mind. Suddenly he burst out:

"Slim, you got any people?" Right away he wished he'd kept his mouth shut. But Slim answered like it didn't matter.

"Yeah, I've got a wife and kids. They live in Rio Gatos, not far from here. Don't see 'em much, bein' as I'm on the trail all the time."

"Don't you miss 'em?"

"Like crazy. What you doin' out here on your own?" Slim pulled a short brown chewing stick out of his shirt pocket and stuck it in his mouth. He gnawed on it thoughtfully.

"Uh . . ." Midnight hesitated. It wasn't shame that stopped him. It was more of a deep sadness, a hurt. *Why did I even bring this up? First black face I see in months, and I start talkin' about all my private business.* Midnight was angry at himself.

Slim spat in the dirt before he spoke again.

"How far did you run?"

Midnight looked away.

Slim eyed him closely. "Oh. Your folks put their lives on the line for you, didn't they? Got *you* out, but only you. First you thought it was good, it was great being FREE. Then you thought about it some more, and decided that maybe without them it ain't so great after all."

Midnight jumped like he'd been hit. It was the truth that hit him hard. "How'd you know that?"

Slim continued. "I know all the signs, kid. I was born in bondage, too. That's a long story for another time. But I'm here to tell you, Midnight. Shake off that bad feeling. What they did, what you did—it *is* worth it. Freedom is worth it all. You made it. Your folks wanted you to make it."

Midnight's mind was spinning. "They saved my life just as much as you did. More." He said it simply, and it was a relief to him. Almost to himself, he whispered, "They gave up any chance they had to run . . . for me."

Slim nodded. "How're you gonna pay them back?" he asked.

"I don't know yet. But I will. I will."

That night, Mississippi Slim ate in the bunkhouse with them. He spoke as much Spanish as he did English, laughing and telling jokes between bites. Midnight found out that Slim was now a trail cook but that he'd been one of the toughest cowhands in west Texas before his back had been hurt in a stampede crossing the Red River. He and Juan Diego had met working on the Crazy Eight Ranch years ago. Mississippi Slim's wife was Juan Diego's cousin. Slim was saving up his money to buy a small farm for his family.

"In a couple of weeks, we start driving about two thousand head of longhorns from the Crazy Eight up a new trail to Kansas. It's a bold move—nobody done it before. If I make it back this will be my last drive," Slim told them.

"I couldn't ever settle down—not me!" Riley shook his head and took a swig of coffee. "This dirt, these sweet cow smells . . . it's all in my blood!" They laughed. Riley began picking a song from his old fiddle.

"Come, Slim!" Juan Diego rose from the table. They stepped out of the bunkhouse. As they walked away, their laughing voices carried back through the darkness.

Midnight wanted to go out with them, but he knew he couldn't. They needed man talk, and although he worked like a man he knew he was still just a kid to them. Midnight lay in his bunk, wishing that he could talk with Slim again before he left. It had been nice, talking to somebody who was like Papa. There was so much more Midnight wanted to ask, to say.

Somebody put the oil lamp out. Juan Diego and Slim still weren't back. Midnight fell asleep.

seven

The next morning, Midnight gulped his coffee and tortillas down quickly. He stepped outside, hoping to catch up with Slim. Slim saw him first.

"Midnight Son!" Slim was leading his spotted pinto out of the corral. "I got a little business talk for you."

"Sure, Slim." Midnight rubbed Dahomey's nose.

"I'm gonna speak plain. We still need a wrangler for the Texas crew. I'll tell you the truth, you won't be ropin' and bronc busting or nothing. Just handling the spare horses on the trail. We call 'em the *remuda*. Cowpokes need to change mounts a few times a day, you know. Juan Diego says you're ready for the job."

Midnight had learned from his time at the ranch that a wrangler's job was the lowest. Still, his heart was thumping with excitement.

"I sure am ready!" he blurted out. Then he thought about what this offer meant. *I'll be leavin' Hacienda de la Suerte. Might never see it again. Gotta go back to Texas, though. If there's a bounty on me . . . but Slim was a slave once. He ain't scared. I guess I gotta learn to live without bein' scared all the time.*

"They've done a lot for me here," Midnight said slowly. "But I'm with you!"

"Then it's a deal. Pay is fair—you get it in a lump at the end of the trail. That works out to a hundred a month for you. We ride as soon as you get your gear."

A hundred dollars. A hundred dollars a month. Sakes alive! I'll be rich!

It took only minutes for Midnight to wrap his few belongings up and meet Slim outside. He was surprised to see the other ranch hands, and he looked around for Juan Diego. The man who had taught him so much was nowhere to be seen.

"Midnight!" Riley stepped out from the group. "You know we ain't much for pretty words and such, but we took quite a liking to you, kid. And now you're goin' off on the trail for the first time. So we all got together and, well, here!"

Baño lifted up a shining leather saddle and placed it gently on Dahomey's back.

"T-th-thanks—" Midnight sputtered. *My own saddle! I can't believe they'd do this for me.*

"It's not new," Riley said. "But we fixed it up and Baño polished it. We figured it'd take you a while to save up for your first saddle." Midnight had lifted his fingers to rub the smooth leather when Juan Diego rode up with Miss Miracles on his horse.

Juan Diego slipped off his horse and grabbed Midnight's hand, shaking it hard. Then he turned it palm-side-up and folded Midnight's fingers around some coins.

"I promised you would be paid once you learned the work. It is not American money—only Mexican pesos. *Vaya con Dios*, Midnight. Go with God."

Midnight didn't have time to think about it. Miss Miracles was handing him something wrapped in a piece of burlap cloth. Midnight shoved the coins into his pocket and dropped his bundle. Miss Miracles laid the package across his arms. Midnight unrolled a deep blue blanket with yellow stripes woven at the ends. He sucked in his breath. He'd seen fancy cloths and blankets hanging on the clothesline back on the plantation, but never up close. This was the most beautiful thing Midnight had ever held in his hands.

"Milagros began weaving this for you the day after we found you," Juan Diego told him. "She says the dark blue is for the midnight skies, and the yellow is for the stars to light your way." Miss Miracles suddenly gave Midnight a big hug. He looked from the saddle to the blanket, at Juan Diego.

"Y'all found me. You taught me ropin', ridin'. I don't know how to pay you back for this."

Juan Diego shook his head. "Some things we do because it is right to do them. We helped you because it was the right thing. You owe us nothing for that."

"I'll always remember," Midnight replied.

"Let's ride, son!" Slim mounted and spurred his horse to a fast trot.

Midnight swung himself up into his saddle. Not too hard, not too stiff. It felt good. He waved his hat.

"Gracias!" he said carefully. *"Ad-adios!"* Miss Miracles was wiping her eyes. The men all flung their hats into the air, calling and yelling in Spanish. Midnight knew he would miss them. He looked over all their faces, painting a picture in his mind. Finally he turned his eyes ahead to Slim, to his new adventure. He dug his heels into Dahomey's sides.

"Here we go again, Dahomey," he said. "But this time, it's good to know where." Dahomey seemed to agree. He broke into a full run.

"Yo!" Midnight whooped. "Yip! Yip, hey, get on up!"

✳

After a three-day ride, Mexico was behind them. Texas was spread out ahead. Midnight had wished for the chance to talk to someone—now he had it. Slim was a talker.

"I been workin' on the Crazy Eight off and on for 'bout eight years," he told Midnight. "It's the ridin' I love."

"That's what I like. Goin' places. I never went more'n a few miles from that old plantation," said Midnight.

"Ain't that a shame. Boy! What a life you got before you now. I bet if more of our folk knew for real how good this free life is, they'd rise up by the thousands and end this slavery thing in a hot minute."

"Thousands?" Midnight questioned.

"What do you think?" Slim answered. "They been bringin' slave ships over that water for a hundred years!" Midnight was shocked into silence. *I never thought about how many of us there must be. Always seemed like we must be outnumbered. How can a handful of folk make thousands of other folk suffer so?*

Midnight mostly listened in these talks, since he didn't have nearly as long a life as Slim's to talk about. Slim told Midnight how he'd started working on the Crazy Eight roping cows during round-ups. Before that he'd been a broncobuster up Denver way.

"I was a wrangler, too." Slim spat at a fly. "You

gotta follow the remuda in the daytime. Find their grazing places. At night, you tie 'em up to pickets that you drive into the ground."

Midnight started feeling very comfortable around Slim. He and Slim got around to discussing everything. That is, almost everything. Slim didn't talk about being a slave. Midnight let that be. After all, he tried hard not to even think about his own past.

"I gotta ask you somethin', Slim," Midnight said one day.

"Ask on, my friend."

"Like you say, I'm gonna get straight to the point. Am I gonna be safe back in Texas?"

Slim slowed his horse and took out his chewing stick. "Ain't no pattyrollers where we're going, Midnight. 'Course, I been a free man for ten years. No pattyroller could take me alive! Believe me, I know the folks at the Crazy Eight. Joe B. owns the place. Me and him go back quite a few years. He don't go along with slavery. And that war has got Texas so torn up that nobody's around to pay reward money if they did catch runaways. White folks who ain't occupied with fightin' are occupied with holding on to their land."

"Yeah, but that don't mean we can't still run into trouble." Midnight looked at Slim.

"Smart man. Black folk in this country can and

will run into trouble any place, any time. Free or slave. Remember that."

"I will," Midnight answered.

Toward dusk that evening, they began to see a few sheds spotting the prairie here and there. Midnight could make out the shadowy shapes of a few cattle in the distance.

"The Crazy Eight's only a couple of miles north. We'll ride on through till daybreak," Slim announced over the campfire when they stopped to eat. Midnight was getting to like Slim's cooking. He carried only his sleeping roll, a double saddlebag, and a cast iron pan, but what he could do with a little food was amazing.

Tonight he stirred up some wild greens he'd picked along with a little piece of dried beef and some herbs that he kept in a muslin pouch around his waist. Then he warmed up some tortillas in the fire ash and boiled a pot of strong coffee. Midnight sat back with his tin plate, holding every bite in his mouth until he had to swallow it to get the next bit in.

"The eatin' has been mighty fine, Slim," Midnight mumbled through his food. "If you cook this good on the trail, it's a wonder the cowpokes can get up on their horses!"

"Well, thank you. It's a gift, this cooking. One

thing I got from my mama before . . ." He stopped, pretending to be busy pouring coffee.

"Never mind," Midnight said softly. "I put my mama away in a far-off place, too. For me and nobody else."

Slim was quiet for a while. In the flickering campfire, Midnight could see that he had smiled.

"Like I said," Slim spoke after a while, "we're real close to the Crazy Eight. No use stopping now. The roundup starts tomorrow. In two or three days all the new livestock will be branded and ready to go. Joe picked up a dozen mustangs a few weeks ago for this drive. Best you get to know your way around the horses."

"Let's hit it!" Midnight helped clean the plates by "washing" them in the hot ashes. Slim packed up.

"This trail we're taking up north is a new one. Started as a supply route for the war," Slim said. "We're gone drive this herd east, just outside of Fort Worth, then pick up the trail north."

"This herd—how many head did you say it's got?" Midnight asked, thinking back.

"Two thousand."

"I don't know much, but ain't that a lot of long-horns to move? Those are some nasty critters!"

Slim laughed. "Nasty, but they can stand the drive. Some of these new breeds folks are bringing in here from all over might be pretty, but they just ain't gonna hold up on a long drive. And once this war is over, cattle is gonna be driven all over the West. You wait and see."

They didn't talk much for the next few hours. Midnight thought about his job. *Wonder what kind of horses I'll be lookin' out for? How many? And I ain't too sure about those other cowboys, either. They're white men. Slim swears they'll be all right.*

"Ho!" Slim suddenly shouted. Midnight squinted. The sun was casting a weak morning light over the flat, grassy ground. Midnight could see ranch buildings and what looked like hundreds of black dots spread out around them. His eyes widened as he and Slim rode closer. What he was looking at were cattle. Longhorns. Hundreds and hundreds of longhorns, as far as he could see.

eight

The Crazy Eight was hopping at sunup. The crew was already branding cattle for the big drive. Everywhere cowboys were yelling as cows bellowed. Some men were on horseback, spinning their lariats in the air. Each man would toss the flying circle around the horns of the nearest steer, pulling it to the ground. Another man would rush out and swiftly tie the animal's forelegs together, holding down its rear. A third pressed the red-hot branding iron onto the howling longhorn's hip, pulling the iron off as quickly as he set it down. In seconds the angry animal was untied and the cowboys were hurrying out of its way.

"We got twelve men on the crew, countin' you, Midnight," Slim said. "Each fella will be changing mounts twice a day."

"So I'll be lookin' after . . ." Midnight was quick at counting, always had been. "About twenty-four horses? That's not countin' your chuck wagon, though."

Slim looked at Midnight for a minute. "You're a fast thinker, son. Juan Diego was right about you. I got four ox pulling my wagon, and my own horse. Here, let me take you to the trail boss and get this deal official." They tied their horses to a hitching post and Slim led the way toward two men who were looking at a map spread over an old stump.

"Joe B.! Found a wrangler at last!"

"Well done, Slim!" Joe B.'s voice boomed over the other noise as he turned to size Midnight up.

"I'm Joe B. Martin, owner and boss of this dust eatin' outfit. 'Round here the men call me Joe B."

"Midnight Son," Midnight said in a strong, clear voice. Joe B. held out his large leathery hand and Midnight shook it. *This don't feel so strange as it did with Riley.*

"This your first drive, Midnight?"

"Yep."

"I trust Mississippi Slim more than any man I know. If he says you can handle this remuda, you got the job. This ain't gonna be easy."

"I know how to work hard," Midnight said quietly. Joe B. grunted.

"I reckon Slim has already told you something

about the job. Handling horses is your number-one duty. Any time you got in between, you'll help Slim however he sees fit. Take a walk down to the corral behind the barn. Check out the ponies. Curly's my supply man. He's sorting gear over there in the shed. Ask him for your bedroll and anything else you need. I'll want to see all the men tonight after chow." Joe B. touched his hat and returned to his map.

Slim popped a new chewing stick into his mouth. "Joe likes to make sure you got all the facts, Midnight."

Midnight nodded. "Yeah. I'm gonna take a look at the ponies." *Gotta be on my own sooner or later,* he thought. *Slim brought me here, but I can't live in his shadow.*

Slim understood right away that Midnight wanted to go alone. "Go on and take care of business. I hafta pack up my chow wagon and go over my supplies anyway."

Midnight turned toward the barn. All around him were the noises of men and animals. The morning sun beat down on his head. As he walked, his boots felt hot and tight. He breathed deeply and slowly, hoping to calm the shaky feeling starting inside his belly. Then he passed the building and saw the horses.

A rusty brown creature with a blue-black mane

✳

trotted right up to him. It was a small female, who bent her strong neck and looked directly into Midnight's eyes.

"Hey there, gal," Midnight whispered, reaching his open hand out. She sniffed at him. He leaned against the fence, draping one arm over. A few other horses seemed to notice him, but they stayed on the other side of the corral. Midnight rubbed the rusty horse's flank. "Red," he said quietly, naming her. She tossed her head and made a sound like a hiss. "All right, then. Rusty." Rusty seemed to nod and Midnight smiled. It had been such a long time since he'd smiled that his face felt strange. He shook his head and eased his body up over the fence to stand inside the corral.

Twelve assorted mustangs. The other horses makin' up the remuda must be the men's own. Remembering Baño's lessons, Midnight moved slowly into the group. He made no noise. He just stood there, silently, for a long time.

The horses ignored him at first. Only Rusty would get close to him and nuzzle his ear. After a while, a spotted black-and-white horse bumped his back gently. Then the others, one by one, accepted him. Midnight stayed in the middle, letting the horses move around him. *Next I'll bring Dahomey in here, see how they take to him. Now, for my gear.* Midnight climbed out of the corral. Rusty followed him and watched as he walked toward a small, faded gray shed. The door was propped open by a tightly sealed barrel. Midnight cleared his throat loudly and stuck his head in.

"Curly? Anybody here? I come for my gear."

A clump of bright red hair shot up from behind some saddles. Sharp green eyes stared out from under the hair. A bushy red mustache and beard hid the mouth.

"Ay! Another Dark Dan, are ye?" His voice boomed in the little space, and the following laughter bounced off Midnight's tight nerves.

Midnight clenched his jaw and made himself stare at the eyes.

"Name's Midnight Son. I'm the new wrangler."

The green eyes narrowed. "Oh, you take me the wrong way, boy. I didn't mean nothing by what I said. Dark Dan is only a . . ."

Midnight called up his courage. "A what? A pet name like you give a dog?"

"You darkies do stick together, doncha? Guess that's why Slim sought ya out."

Midnight was angry. He'd been angry at white men before. The anger was old and powerful. But slaves couldn't do anything about that. The anger was rolling up hot inside him and he wanted to get away fast. *He's workin' my last nerve! And I can't mess things up on the first day by causin' trouble. Slim's countin' on me. I gotta keep my head straight.*

Midnight spoke quietly. "I need a bedroll and a couple of coils of rope for tetherin' the horses."

"I don't hold nothing against your kind . . ." Curly kept trying to explain as he stacked Midnight's supplies. "I mean, I heard you darkies were lazy, no-good. From what I've seen, though, you people do the work of ten mules . . ."

Midnight grabbed the supplies off the floor and spun around, his legs making the longest strides they could to get away. Curly was still talking.

Why won't he hush up? Or is he tryin' to make me mad, make me do somethin' so I'll get thrown off the crew? Midnight stopped and stood for a minute. Then he turned, fastened a gaze, and stared. He stared with hot gray eyes at the cool green ones, his anger flying past those eyes, down, down, into that body, into that heart. Midnight's anger struck hard, and Curly staggered back. His feet suddenly seemed unsteady. Midnight widened his eyes, then without blinking slowly moved his head around. He heard Curly muttering as he walked away.

After his run-in with Curly, Midnight filled the day with better things. He took Dahomey down to the corral and left him with the ponies. He practiced his knot-tying with the new rope to make sure his double knots would hold tight when he tethered the horses on the trail. He'd helped Slim pack food supplies and barrels of water into the wagon he'd fixed up just for trail drives. Joe B. had asked Midnight to help with the branding, so he'd worked with two other cowboys to hold down steers and cows for the branding iron.

Night rolled around. By the time Slim shook the loud old cowbell to call the men to eat, Midnight was feeling like he was a part of the team.

Slim did himself proud. He had cooked outside, so the smells had been teasing everyone all day. When they lined up to get their tin plates filled, Slim spooned out steaming mounds of thick chicken stew. Midnight breathed in the delicious smell. There were hunks of carrots, potatoes, and meat swimming in a thick, spicy gravy. Plopped beside the stew were two of the biggest buttery biscuits Midnight had ever seen.

Like all the other men, Midnight huddled over his food and shoveled it down.

"We got apple cobbler and hot coffee with chickory over here, boys!" Slim smiled wide as there was a scramble for his makeshift plank table. Joe B. swallowed down his coffee and stood beside the table as the others had their sweet treat.

✳

83

"Well, men, here we sit full as ticks on Mississippi Slim's good eatin'." The men mumbled and nodded their agreement. Joe B. went on.

"I tell you this man is an inspiration over a fryin' pan and a campfire, but we know about that. We been down the trail before together. All except for the new wrangler, Midnight Son here." He looked toward Midnight, and all the men looked at him, too.

"We ain't fancy around here, Midnight. So lemme just tell you who the rest of the fellas are. There's Jake, Andy, Lone Eagle, Pablo. Kid's here, Big Lou and Lou Boy, and Curly." Curly looked into his coffee cup.

Midnight noticed a few things about some of the others: Jake wore all black; Lone Eagle wore two long braids and a red bandanna tied around his head. Lou Boy seemed only a little older than Midnight and must be Big Lou's son 'cause they had the same long chin.

Joe B. went on. "All right. This trail we're heading on is raw. Right now it's being used to haul war supplies. That ain't my concern. But the railroad is comin' through Kansas, and I got a contract to sell beef to the railroad company for the work crew. All we got to do is get this herd to Wyandotte County. I can't tell you what we're up against." He paused and spat into the dirt near his foot.

"I got a mixed herd here, bulls, steers, and cows. Might get dicey along the way if the cows drop calves, but I plan to make it to Kansas in three months. I don't want to push the cattle any more than we have to." He took a swig of the coffee that Slim handed him silently.

"Midnight, you and the remuda travel up ahead with Slim and his chow wagon. The rest of us follow with the herd. I want Jake and Big Lou in front, on point. Curly, Andy, and Pablo flank the herd. Lone Eagle, Lou Boy, and Kid are behind on drag."

"Say, Joe B., ain't we gonna run into twister season on this?" Kid frowned.

"Yeah. But it's a risk we hafta take. This is April. The man wants beef by July, latest. At the price per head that we agreed on, this trip will be more than worth it for all of us."

The men mumbled and nodded again. Midnight took this to mean that they trusted Joe B.'s word about the money.

"One last thing." Joe B. looked at Midnight for a minute, then off into the night sky. "I'm gonna say this one time. On my crew, I'm the boss. I expect my men to back each other up. And I expect you all to do whatever it takes to get this herd to Wyandotte on its feet. Slim, first call is at sunup day after tomorrow. We head out immediately after chow."

With that, he strode off toward the bunkhouse. The others slowly finished their coffee and broke off into pairs or huddled in threes. Midnight got up to take his cup over to Slim. Lou Boy got up with him.

"Midnight?" Lou Boy's voice was high-pitched and scratchy. Midnight turned to him. He had an honest, wide-open face. His eyes were dark. His hair was long and mousy brown, hanging across one eye. He pushed the hair back behind his ear, and Midnight noticed a little brown beard stubble on his long chin.

"Yeah?"

"Thanks for helping out with that branding. Them longhorns can be mighty mean."

"Um-hmm." Midnight wanted to answer, "Don't I know it!" and sit down with Lou Boy to ask him all about what he did. But something stopped him from speaking. Something stopped him from feeling easy and kindhearted to this boy who was trying to be nice. Part of Midnight wanted to fight that something inside himself, because it made him feel just about as mean as those old longhorns. Curly had brought out that *other* part—that fence in his mind that he'd set up long, long ago between himself and the people who'd hurt him most . . . white people.

Lou Boy didn't seem to notice anything hurtful in the way Midnight talked. He held up his cup for

Slim to fill it and leaned on the chow wagon to talk some more.

"This your first trail?"

"Yeah."

"Man, there's nothing like bein' out there, just you and the sky and the sun and the animals, with all God's country stretched out around you!" Now that idea tugged at Midnight's heart. Lou Boy sounded like he felt the same as Midnight had felt in those days when he was on the run.

"It's the freedom, ain't it?" Midnight had to say. Lou Boy looked at him and smiled, shaking his head. "You know it!" he answered.

Midnight was surprised at how close Lou Boy's words were to his own thinking. They didn't speak anymore, but they both stood there, looking out at the blue-black sky peppered with white stars. Slim seemed to clean up silently, so the only sounds surrounding them were crickets chirping in the bushes.

nine

Two mornings later, Mississippi Slim was packing the last of the cooking pots he'd used to make breakfast. "Mornin', Midnight! Can you help me load this last water barrel before you go down to the corral?" Midnight was headed to the corral already, but he swung around and smiled at his friend.

"Can't believe it's 'bout to begin, Slim! I'm really gonna ride the trail!"

Slim chuckled as they heaved the sloshing barrel up onto the back of the chow wagon. "Calm down, puppy dog. I been on many a trail in my lifetime, and nothin's harder than a new one. We don't know what's out there." Slim grunted and tightened heavy ropes around the barrel to keep it in place when the wagon started moving. Midnight frowned.

"You mean wildcats, Indians . . ."

"I mean that, and also floods, bad water or *no* water, twisters . . ."

"We'll get the cattle through, Slim. Ain't nothin' gonna stop Midnight's first drive!" Midnight grinned and touched his hat, heading off.

Dahomey met him at the corral gate.

"Hey there." Midnight let the horse nuzzle his shoulder. He rubbed the horse's nose and climbed over the fence. The other ponies gathered around the water trough as Midnight pumped it full. Then he opened the back gate and the animals ran into the pasture to eat. Midnight went into the barn to get his gear.

He silently checked things off as he touched them. Four tight coils of rope for tethering. Eight pickets, the wooden sticks he'd pound into the ground to hold the ropes. He lifted up the small, heavy hammer and swung it around a few times to feel it in his hands. It was a good weight. He had a new coiled whip. A stiff brush for manes and tails. Midnight smiled at this. Back at the plantation, he'd used a brush almost like this to make the horses look fancy. Now he'd only have time to brush out burrs or thorns that the horses might trot through.

He moved on to look at his saddle. There were places on it for all the gear; he double-checked them to make sure nothing was loose. On one side was a special hook for his bundle of belongings. He'd rolled up Miss Miracles' blanket and tied it down on the back. He gently touched the braided leather of his lariat, which he'd also coiled and planned to sling right over his saddle horn.

Midnight felt for his water gourd. *Better fill this now.* He used the edge of a fingernail to carefully pry out the wooden stopper from the small, curved gourd.

I remember when Mama picked this off the vine. She cut off the top and sat it in the sun for weeks to dry out, and Papa showed me how to carve this top from a piece of scrap wood. He pumped water slowly into the narrow mouth of the gourd till it was full, then put the stopper tightly back in place. For a moment, he held the gourd up and turned it around in his hands, feeling his mother and father around him.

A small noise, maybe from the horses or maybe from his mind, made Midnight suddenly swing the leather cord of the gourd around his neck and end his memory just as quickly as it had come.

He whistled for Dahomey. "Hey, boy, you ready?" Dahomey galloped up from the pasture and stood waiting. Midnight slung the saddle over the horse's shining black flanks and carefully cinched it in place. He mounted and rode into the clump of mustangs.

"Yo, ponies, let's go!" Midnight cracked the whip above the heads of the horses and spurred Dahomey forward toward the open gate. Twenty animals nosed ahead, following Midnight and Dahomey's lead. Midnight kept looking around, trying to make sure that the mustangs were coming along. He and Dahomey fell back a bit so that Midnight could pull a few straying ponies in with the group.

Everyone else was moving into place. Midnight could see Slim up on the chow wagon, stowing some last minute bundles underneath the seat. Slim looked up.

"I see you got them ponies in your power!"

"I don't know if I got them in my power, but at least I got 'em movin'!" Slim and Midnight both laughed, and Midnight crowded his ponies around the wagon. He turned in his saddle and looked back.

Joe B. rode a black-and-white pony with a white mane. He trotted back and forth barking out orders. Curly and Andy were raising dust far off to the left, herding the cattle in toward the group that Big Lou and Jake already had standing directly behind the horses. Pablo was coming in from the right, cracking his whip at four bellowing bulls who wanted to go their own way. A flood of cattle was still pouring out from the pasture with Lou Boy riding in the middle of them and Kid far behind. When Lou Boy looked up and saw Midnight, he grinned and waved. Midnight nodded and waved back.

Two thousand cattle shook their heads and

rubbed against one another. Midnight was amazed that so few people could handle such a job. It didn't seem possible that they could force these big animals to move as one, to keep them moving for hundreds of miles!

At the plantation, there were fifty of us in the cotton field alone. And cotton don't move, cotton can't butt you or spear your gut with a two-foot horn. Midnight shook his head at the wonder of it all. *Aw, but in that field it felt like I was shackled to that sack on my back, and the whip was in somebody else's hands, not mine.*

Midnight looked down at the whip that he clutched in his hand. Because he had seen so many men and women beaten to the ground with just such a thing, he knew that he could never hit an animal with this one. He had practiced many a time at Hacienda de la Suerte with the whip, learning to bring his arm up high enough to pop the leather up and out instead of down on the backs of the cattle. The cows and horses still seemed to get the idea.

Joe B. passed Midnight from the rear of the herd, giving the boy a nod as he went. Midnight took this as a sign to snap to duty. He sat up as tall as he could in his saddle and reined Dahomey around to face the wagon.

Now Midnight could only see Slim, Joe B., sitting rod-straight, and miles and miles of land ahead.

He smelled the dew, which still clung to the low scrub bushes that dotted the dusty ground. He smelled the animal scent all around, but stronger even than that was the fresh, open air. Free air.

Joe B. spoke some words to Slim that were so quiet Midnight couldn't make them out. Midnight was curious about them being friends. It was pretty clear that Joe B. trusted all the men, but Mississippi Slim was the one he sat up late at night with. Mississippi Slim was the one who knew Joe B.'s business but never opened his mouth about it. Joe B. knew all about Slim's plans to buy a farm, and about his family.

It almost seems like it don't matter that the two of them is as different as night and day. 'Course, the way the world is made, you can't have night without day and day can't dawn if there ain't no night. As Midnight smiled at his own strange, wonderful thought, Joe B.'s voice rang out.

"FORWARD—HOOOO!" Joe B. flipped off his yellow felt hat and swirled it around his head. He spurred his horse and galloped off. Slim yelled at his oxen and the wagon lurched ahead. Giving Dahomey's reins the lightest pull and following, Midnight glanced behind.

The river of horns and bony backs flowed along, spreading out and away like a flood topping its banks. The trail drive had started.

When the sun had rolled up to the middle of the sky, Joe B. was traveling on at least a half hour beyond Midnight and Slim. Midnight and Slim were way ahead of the herd, too. Big Lou and Jake, the closest of the others, looked like bugs crawling along the backs of one big moving animal.

Midnight had spent the hours inside himself, thinking hard about keeping the horses together. He and Dahomey moved from the front to the back of the remuda, then circled around the outside to force any stragglers in. Midnight hadn't allowed himself to take his mind off his duty.

"Midnight!" Slim broke into his quiet. "We're gonna noon up ahead about a mile so's I can get chow and the herd can graze. The boys'll change horses. There's a stream for the animals to get water."

Midnight nodded and wondered for a minute how Slim knew there was a stream up ahead. Then he realized that this part of the trail was old stuff to all of them; they still had to pass Fort Worth before they veered off onto the newer part of the trail.

The nooning meal was fast, and Midnight's was faster than everyone else's. He gobbled down the beans and hoecake, then hurried back to his horses. One by one, the cowboys swung off their tired animals with their saddles in hand. Midnight watched as each man quickly slung his saddle onto a fresh horse and rejoined the herd in minutes. Midnight barely had time to send off one hot, thirsty pony to the stream before the next man galloped up. Everything happened at once. Some men stayed with the cattle; some wolfed down food; some changed horses and galloped back to their places with the herd. In an hour nooning was all finished and they were back on the move.

After that first morning Midnight had to start over again keeping the new horses in line. That pretty Rusty which he'd made friends with yesterday didn't seem to feel that she should do what all the other horses did today. Midnight edged Dahomey right up beside her.

"Now, look, Rusty." Midnight drank a swig of water from his gourd and eyed the trotting pony carefully. He didn't raise his voice.

"You ain't gonna cause me problems on my first day out, are you?" The pony shook her mane and snorted. Midnight laughed.

"Oh, you aimin' to be the boss, are you? Well, there's just one boss of this here remuda, Rusty. I'm it. You do good by me and I'll do good by you. That's my promise."

Rusty wouldn't look at him, but she fell into step with Dahomey. Midnight was satisfied. He rode along with her for a while, then felt like talking to another person. Slowly he and Dahomey moved toward the head of the remuda, near Slim's wagon.

Slim knew Midnight was there without even looking back. "Them ponies are a handful, right, Midnight Son?"

Midnight grinned. Slim was beginning to know what he was thinking, almost before he thought it. *It's kind of like Papa is sittin' up there on that wagon. What would Papa think of all this, anyway?* Midnight only wondered about that for a second. He knew the answer. *Papa always wanted me to be able to go where I wanted when I wanted. This is where I wanna be.*

"I don't understand how you got to know me so good in this short time, Mississippi Slim."

"I was born with a double veil, son. Means I can read people like other folks read words in books. I can feel what folks are thinkin' without being told."

"So what am I thinkin' right now?" Midnight teased him, riding up so he could look into Slim's squinting face.

Slim turned slowly to look at the boy, and a smile crept across his face as he did.

"You're thinkin': This old man is sun crazy and we ain't halfway to Kansas."

Midnight burst into laughter. "Naw!"

Slim laughed too. But he didn't say what he was reading in Midnight's face. He never did say.

ten

When Joe B. halted the herd for the day, Midnight had already spotted a grassy flat spot northeast of the camp. *The horses hafta be tied good and tight through the night. I've gotta drive these pickets down solid into the ground. That's a good place, not too many rocks. Firm ground to hold the stakes when I get 'em in.*

He tied Dahomey to the chow wagon, took out his tools, and set to work. He pounded his first picket into the hard ground, working up a sweat. He used the toe of his boot to nudge the picket. It didn't move. He marked off twenty paces from the picket and drove another one down. Next, he knotted and double-knotted one end of his coiled rope around the first picket. He stretched the rope and pulled it, checking again to make sure the picket was secure in the ground. Finally he looped and tied the end of the rope to the second picket, knotting it carefully.

Then he went over to Rusty, who was nibbling some sweet grass. She seemed to be the leader, and when she moved, the others moved too. One by one Midnight tethered six ponies to the picket line.

He worked on, not paying attention to anyone or anything else. Sweat rolled down his temples. He licked the salty taste off his lips and kept going. Six more. At last he tied Dahomey to the line and stood to wipe his forehead. Midnight looked back at the work he'd done. The horses hadn't really given him any trouble. His first day on the drive was over, and he was satisfied.

"Good job for your first time." Joe B. strolled up and tugged on the last rope line Midnight had stretched. It was so tight that the rope bounced against Joe's hand. He nodded and looked at Midnight.

"Looks like you need a cooldown, son."

"Sure could use it," Midnight said, still wiping sweat from his neck.

"Well, now that you're out of the saddle for the day, you can take it easier. Pablo and Big Lou are on duty tonight, patrolling the edges of the herd for trouble. We call it night herding. They'll get fresh mounts right after chow. If Slim don't need you for anything, you're a free man till wake-up. But remember, you stand guard over these ponies." Joe

B. walked off just like he had come, with his thumbs hung in his pants pockets and his hat pushed back on his head. Midnight realized that he'd never seen the big man move suddenly, or fast.

Bet that don't mean he couldn't beat a deer in a footrace. Midnight chuckled to himself and walked down a low ridge to the pond. He gulped a handful of water, threw some of it up onto his face, and sat back on his haunches.

Midnight looked all around. Texas land was mostly flat with a few ridges. This part of the country had more wild grass and ground cover than the West. Some low hills rose up here and there. Beyond them, the sky was stripes of pink and yellow and orange behind the dull blaze of the setting sun.

I'm a free man till wake-up call, Joe B. says. Well, well. A man who could be my master has told me I'm free. Ain't that like a fox passin' up a chicken house. This new life is somethin' else.

Midnight stretched his legs, then his arms. Sniffing the air, he caught the smell of sowbelly and beans. He scrambled up and made his way to the chow wagon.

"Well, here's the horse man!" Mississippi Slim was standing over a steaming kettle, his ladle dripping onto Lou Boy's already full plate. Lou Boy snatched a handful of fried bread and hungrily slopped it into the creamy mound of white beans.

"Better hurry up, Midnight! Slim's beans and bacon go faster'n a mad bull chasin' a tenderfoot cowhand!"

✳

99

"I sure hope that tenderfoot cowhand ain't me!" Midnight felt easy around Slim and Lou Boy. He got his plate filled, too. Slim gave him a quick, private look with his eyebrows raised, like he was asking if everything was really all right. Midnight just raised his chin a little, with a smile. Slim moved his eyes on to the next cowpoke in line, telling Pablo he'd better watch how much he was eating, or his horse would end up bowlegged.

"First day go all right?" Lou Boy mumbled through his food.

"Mmmm." Midnight swallowed. "Didn't see hide or hair of you."

"Man, them cattle spread out so far that I was miles behind. All the dust they kick up, it's a wonder I could see myself!" They both laughed. Midnight watched the others get food and gather around the fire where the coffeepot was bubbling. He watched Curly among them, carefully sitting so he wasn't looking in Midnight's direction.

Midnight snorted. *That man truly can't stand no black folk.* Lou Boy looked up and noticed where Midnight was looking, but he said nothing. Midnight ate faster than he wanted to. He had to get away before Lou Boy asked any questions about Curly.

"Lemme get on over to check the remuda," Midnight spoke as he poured himself a cup of coffee. "Need me for anything?" He stacked his plate on the plank table near the chow wagon. Slim was perched on the open back of the wagon, chewing on a stick.

"Naw." He watched Midnight take a swig from his tin cup. "Listen. You need to give up whatever you're holding against Curly. If a man ain't insulted your mama or your wife, it ain't worth the trouble on the trail."

Midnight couldn't answer. It was too fresh in his mind. *Curly's the type who'd just as soon turn me in for money as look at me.*

"Maybe later," he called over his shoulder to Slim, walking away.

"Later ain't always soon enough!" Slim near-whispered into the darkness.

Midnight said goodnight to Dahomey, then walked among the other horses. Nighttime made him think of being on the run. He hunched his shoulders and tuned his ears in to the sounds around him. An owl hooted somewhere. Then there were only crickets and stillness. There was no danger out here tonight, for his horses or himself.

There was a pattern to it all. The days were long. Riding for so many hours was hard. Grit and dirt lay on the men's clothes, skin, and hair. They traveled under the scorching sun. They sloshed through rain. Only the weather changed. Otherwise, each day was like another.

Midnight liked it because even though he thought he knew what to expect, something unexpected could happen at any time. A cow might decide to have a calf. Slim might spot wild quail and go off on a hunt. A swollen creek might cause them to go miles out of the way to find an easier crossing.

Soon enough they had skirted Fort Worth. Within days they were nearing the border between Texas and Indian territory. This was their first big river crossing.

The mighty Red River seemed to sneak up on them; one day there was only land before them and the next day the ground turned to red clay hills sloping down to all that water. Midnight had never seen so much water in his life.

Joe B. decided to cross the river right then and bed down for the night once the whole herd cleared the other side. Unlike before, he now rode with the men and the herd. Midnight sat tall in Dahomey's saddle and listened hard.

"Midnight, I want you to follow tight behind Slim. This is an easy crossing place, but we can't afford to have any ponies taking a bad step on the riverbed and breaking a leg. Once you're over, you're gonna ride about five miles north. Picket the remuda there and help Slim set up. Got it?"

"Right." Midnight set his lips and took one last turn around his horses, first moving silently like he had that very first day. Then he leaned into them and spoke in a low voice. "Stay with me, now, ponies. Stay with me." Slowly he headed Dahomey up to lead them splashing into the river.

The water rushed beneath them. Crossing against the strong current was like pushing a solid tree trunk. Dahomey nosed forward. Midnight looked from side to side, keeping count. Water was up to the top of his boots. Water rose up to his knees. Midnight felt his fear rising, too. He'd never been in a river, never in any water this deep.

Gotta keep my mind on these horses. I know I can't control no river. Gotta beat this fear down. Midnight dug his heels into Dahomey's sides.

"Come on, ponies! Get along! Get!" His voice rang out. The horses plunged ahead, staying body to body and straining against the water.

"Stay on 'em, Midnight Son!" Slim's voice cheered him on. "Almost to the riverbank! Almost there!"

Midnight dared to look up from the animals. Slim was right.

"All right, ponies! Up we go!"

Dahomey splashed up onto the riverbank and the others scrambled behind. Midnight patted Dahomey's neck.

"We did it, Dahomey," he said quietly. "We did it."

Slim turned his wagon and led Midnight, Dahomey, and the sputtering remuda to the campsite.

eleven

That night, weariness was in Midnight's bones. He felt as if he'd carried every horse over that river on his own back. He was so tired that he didn't even remember what Slim's dinner meal was or tasted like. When he fell into sleep, it was on the bare ground. His still-tied-up bedroll was under his head.

Midnight dreamed. His dream was one of noises: the plantation noises, his family's voices, Spanish talking, water gurgling, and horses splashing. He tossed and turned. But then there was another noise.

"AAAAAAaaaaaaaaaaahhhheeeeee!" Midnight's eyes flew open. Sounded like a woman's scream, but Midnight knew that wasn't it. He sat up, and in the darkness he could see Joe B. doing the same, only with his rifle in hand. Without turning his head, Joe B. hissed, "Shhhhh!"

"AAAAAAAaaaaaaaaahhheeeeee!" Where was it? The sound wasn't loud. Still, it was clear and too close to let any man sleep easy. Other heads popped up.

"Slim!" Joe B. called out in a hoarse whisper. "Check out the rear. I'll handle up here." Midnight quickly loosened a mottled gray horse from the picket. Slim didn't wait for a saddle.

"Think it's a bobcat?" Midnight asked.

"Doggone right," Slim muttered. "Sure don't need no cougars 'round here," he said as he sped off. Joe B. mounted his own horse and followed. He'd said he would pay extra if the entire herd got to Wyandotte. But a cougar could pick them off, one by one, just for sport, if he was evil enough.

The crew sat restless in the dark for two hours, listening to the night. The cougar's call didn't come again. No rifle shot came either. When Slim and Joe B. rode in together, their faces were tight, their jaws clenched. Midnight guessed that the bobcat was still out there somewhere. He checked the horses once more before spreading out his bedroll and lying on it. The sleeping he did after that was so light that he could hear the horses' heavy breathing. A cat stalking a herd was big trouble, and they all knew it.

For nearly a week the cat made itself known by wailing off somewhere in the night, but nobody could spot it. They moved the few calves away from the outer edges of the herd. Joe put two more men on night duty. Nobody slept. On the sixth night, Joe B. stationed Midnight between the remuda and the left flank of the herd. Midnight took his spot an hour or so after chow. He didn't bother to lie down. He propped his back against a smooth rock. The air was cool and still. Midnight huddled in his blanket. He dozed. . . . Suddenly, trouble called.

"Grrrrrr . . . " The growl was low, close. Every man froze. Midnight remembered his nights on the run. That fear of every sound, every movement in the dark except his own came back to him fast. But with the fear came a strength. Darkness was also Midnight's old friend. His sight was as sharp now as it was at midday.

Midnight relaxed his shoulders and stretched his neck upward, looking toward the cattle. *Nothin' there. Wait! Somethin's close to me.* He felt the heat of another living creature. Only a few feet away, the cougar passed him. It passed right by the herd.

Sly animal. It's after the horses. Midnight watched the cougar leap silently upon another rock nearer the remuda. The animals sensed him. They began to sputter and shuffle. Midnight rolled out of his blanket. *I ain't got a weapon in sight,* he thought, crawling backward behind another rock. *If I was smart,*

I'd double-back to camp. But I'm gettin' paid to keep these horses safe. Anything could happen if I leave it like this. 'Sides, I ain't never called myself smart.

The cougar was young, maybe on one of its first hunts. Clearly, it had its eyes on a particular horse, and it was stalking the animal. The cougar paced along the picket rope, moving around in a circle. Midnight tried to follow with his own eyes in the direction the cat's eyes were fixed. *It was Rusty!* Now Midnight couldn't turn away.

I been in this position too many times. When Nile died, I couldn't do nothin'. Lady got pulled outta my own arms, and I couldn't do nothin'. How can I leave poor Rusty at the mercy of this wild thing? She's the first horse in this whole remuda that took a likin' to me.

Midnight felt his muscles tighten. *Gotta have a weapon.* He scrambled around on the ground, looking for a stick, a rock, anything that he could use. His foot went down on something hard, and he reached for it. A square-shaped brown stone glinted in the moonlight. Midnight picked it up, weighing it with his hand. It was heavy, maybe as large as his palm.

If I can throw it right at his temple, I can bring him down. Midnight nodded to himself. He had a plan. He crawled closer, ready to spring up and throw in one movement. The cat flattened its whole body against

✷
107

the rock, even laying back its ears. Ready to pounce at any minute.

Midnight drew back his arm and jumped up. The cat suddenly turned its head and saw him. Midnight flung the rock. The cat sprang at him. Midnight twisted his body away as he fell down, feeling the cat dig its claws into his shoulder.

"Yow!" Midnight yelled. Pain shot through his arm and neck, but he managed to force his elbow back into the animal's ribs.

"AAAAaaaaahhhhheeeee!" the cat screamed. Midnight could feel the warm blood running down his chest from his shoulder. *Awww, bobcat. You're not gonna kill ME tonight!* The cat spun around and jumped back toward Midnight's face. This time, Midnight grabbed at the cat's throat. The animal snarled, batting its paws out to strike Midnight wherever he could. They tussled and wrestled and rolled. First Midnight was on top, then they flipped around. The cat was on top, but he'd gotten turned belly up. With his good arm, Midnight managed to grab hold of the scruff of the cat's neck, yanking its head back with all his strength.

"Midnight! Get clear!" He heard Joe B., but he couldn't let go. The cat twisted, digging its back claws into Midnight's stomach. The new pain made Midnight's anger come up. The anger he had pushed aside for Curly. The anger he had buried deep inside for Lady. It was all back. The anger got bigger and hotter. Like a wave passing over him, Midnight's arms, legs, and shoulders began to tremble with anger that was bubbling up.

Midnight shot out his bleeding arm and locked his hand around one of the cat's hind legs.

"YEEEE!" The cat squealed and wriggled, but Midnight couldn't, wouldn't let go. He still clutched the animal's neck, feeling its hot breath as it jerked its head from side to side. He could hear the men shouting at him, but they sounded far, far away.

This is like some kind of dream . . . or nightmare. If I let go now, this madness might take over me and I'll die. I gotta get rid of it.

The pain in his shoulder and stomach burned like fire, but the boiling anger gave Midnight a power he'd never known before. With a strength he didn't know he had, he raised the cat over his head and flung him like a rag into the night.

"AWWWWWWWWWW!" the cat howled, and three men took off after it. Midnight slumped to the ground, breathing hard. *The pain is somethin' terrible, but the anger is all gone.* He smiled, and that was how they found him.

✳

———•—•———

Midnight heard voices in the distance
"He's hurt!"

"Boy, that cat knows he's been in a fight!"

"Why didn't you wait for a gun?"

"I ain't never seen nothin' like that before!"

Midnight tried to sit up but sprawled backward. "I'm all right. I—I just did it for the remuda, that's all. Wasn't smart, but I did it." Midnight was bloody and still panting, but all he felt was calm.

Slim appeared with a handful of thick green leaves and a small bottle.

"Boy, I believe your heart was bigger than your brain this time. What possessed you to jump that cat like that?" He tore open Midnight's shirt. The bobcat's claws had already ripped it pretty badly.

"The red mustang . . . " Midnight was suddenly very tired. "I had to do somethin' this time . . ."

"What? Whatcha mean, this time?" Slim was tearing the shirt up to make a bandage.

Midnight lowered his voice. The other cowboys were still stomping through the brush a distance away. "When my sister got sold, she was snatched right outta my hands, and I . . . I couldn't do nothin'. I figured I could *do* somethin' this time." Slim looked at him thoughtfully.

"So you got mad, huh? Cats and horses ain't people, Midnight. You can't go 'round, savin' up madness till it blows up on you. You lucked out this time. People like us can't always let our bad memories rule us. Hmmm. You got cut up pretty bad, all right. This shoulder's clawed kinda deep."

He broke one of the leaves in half, and a thick juice oozed out over Midnight's skin. It was cool. "This here's aloe. It's a healing plant. I'll rub it in and bandage you up. The pain is gonna be rough before it gets better, but I'll put some more aloe on in the morning. Rest easy, now." Midnight had already closed his eyes.

He heard Joe B.'s voice. "The cat's long gone. Won't trouble this herd no more. And I hope this kid won't take no more crazy chances, either. You told me he was ready, Slim."

Slim grunted. "Midnight wasn't fighting no bobcat, Joe B. He was fighting somethin' none of us could see."

twelve

Midnight couldn't ride for two days. Lou Boy had to take care of the remuda while Midnight was laid out in the back of the chow wagon with his head on flour sacks. He felt like his whole body had been beaten. The aloe worked just as Slim said it would. Two weeks later, Midnight carried scars over his arm, shoulder, and stomach to remind him of the fight, and a throbbing when he lifted his right arm.

Some of the other men reminded him almost every day of his deed. Lou Boy kept talking about it.

"So, Midnight! What was it like lookin' into that critter's yellow eyes?" He'd start up almost every night at chow. Midnight would just shake his head. Pablo would laugh. Andy had started a song about it, which he'd half-sing, half-moan over the campfire. Jake picked out a good and mournful tune on his fiddle to go with the words.

Oh, that bobcat turned tail and run,
'Cause he got whipped by a cowboy called . . .
Midnight Son. . . .

Lone Eagle and Big Lou sat back in the shadows
smiling when they weren't on night herd. Slim
hummed and cleared away his pots and pans. Curly
took care to stay clear of it all. Except for one night,
weeks later, when Midnight got up to go check the
remuda.

He could hear the last strains of Jake's whining
strings as he came up on Curly, staring off at the
stars. Midnight didn't like being surprised from behind, and he figured that nobody else appreciated
it, either. But he still had a hard spot in his heart
for Curly. So he stepped right up to Dahomey and
the horse snorted. Curly jumped and turned at the
same time.

"You could get yourself killed, sneakin' up on a
lad like that!" Curly snarled in his odd-sounding
voice. Slim had told Midnight that Curly was from
a place across the ocean called Ireland. Said that
Curly's people didn't have it so good over there,
starving and all. That should've made Midnight
soften his own feelings, but it didn't. *How can a man
who's been under somebody's thumb with nothin' to his name
treat another fellow like dirt?*

"I ain't up for fightin' no bobcats tonight,"

✳

Midnight said, walking along his tethered rope. He bent to check it for tightness.

"You think you're somethin' for acting the fool, do you? I was beginnin' to think you might have some smarts till you fought a wildcat!" Curly folded his arms across his chest.

So, after all this time of avoidin' me, Curly's ready to go face to face. In the dark. Ha! Somethin' mighty funny about this, Midnight thought. He straightened up and folded his arms the same way.

"I don't think I'm somethin' for tusslin' with that cat. It was a crazy thing to do. But if you wanna know, I think I'm somethin' 'cause I *am* somethin', same as you."

"Listen, Dan . . ."

"Don't call me Dan, or Dark Dan, or Blackie, or nothin' that ain't my name. I ain't never called you Red." Midnight tensed his muscles and waited.

Curly snorted. "So you expect me to treat you special 'cause you were in bondage, do ya?"

"Special?" Midnight dropped his arms and stared through the night, not believing what he'd heard. *"Special?"* he repeated. "This is treatin' me special? Throwin' my gear at me, so you don't have to touch my hands? Spittin' out them made-up names you call me?" Midnight felt himself getting hot. He remembered what Slim had said. *Can't always let memories rule us.*

Curly sighed. "I been workin' like an ox since I come to this country, and I got nothin' to show for it. And you . . . " He stopped. "You people . . . you get free and act as if you own the world, when you own nothin', came from nothin'. I don't understand it!"

Midnight said quietly, "I own myself now, don't you see? And that's the world to me. Bad as it was where you come from, nobody never *owned* you, did they? When you got sick of it, you up and left. Didn't nobody come after you with dogs, did they? Or beat your mama for nursin' your baby brother?" Midnight trembled as those words came out. He hadn't meant for them to, but they did anyway.

Curly shook his head slowly. "I never saw a black before I came here. I always heard . . ."

"Stop there. What *you* heard can't be near as bad as what I've heard to my face."

Curly laughed nervously. "That's the truth of it, I guess."

"Slim told me some things about you, where you come from. And the truth of it is that we really ain't that much different, you and me."

Curly looked straight at Midnight for the first time. "I suppose I have to leave behind what I heard and open my eyes to what I see."

Midnight looked at him. *What's he tryin' to say, that he wants to change, now? How can I believe that? He coulda opened his eyes a long time ago, when he called me Dark Dan before he even asked me my name. Well, I'm not ready yet.*

"Some nice words now don't change the way you talked to me before," Midnight said.

Curly shrugged. "It's up to you, then, isn't it?" he said quietly.

Midnight shook his head. "No, I think it's up to you. Show me that you mean what you say."

"Maybe," Curly muttered. He wandered back to the camp. Midnight stretched his legs out on the ground, then lay back to look directly up at the sky.

What a way I have come. You, Moon, and your sister, Sun, have surely helped me out. Can't believe I'm out here, choosin' how to live my life. If only Papa could see me, be out here with me. He wuz always sayin', "Us all got created to live the best we can." Papa knew all along that slavin' wasn't the best for us. He would tell me to give thanks to my Creator now. I'm free.

"Thank you," Midnight whispered to the stars. "I'm not livin' the best I can yet, but I'm close. I'm close, and I'm tryin'."

———

The next day Midnight noticed the sky again as he untied the horses. His fingers kept fumbling because the animals were restless, straining against the ropes. When he set them off, they milled around in a funny way. Midnight coiled his rope. *Somethin' in the weather is gonna change,* he thought. Overhead the sky was still clear and bright blue. But far off in the distance, where the sky and the low hills seemed to meet, the color looked strange. The clouds were almost gone and they'd left a purple-gray glow in their place.

"Midnight!" Joe B. suddenly rode up, red in the face and breathing hard.

"Bad storm comin' from the east. Slim's got some oilcloth ponchos. Grab one for yourself and get those horses moving. We've got a couple of deep gullies about three miles up, and I want to clear them before we get the worst of the storm. Otherwise, my herd and my money is gonna wash right out from under me." He sped on toward the rear, shouting orders to the others. Midnight rode ahead. Slim had stretched a tight piece of oilcloth over the chow wagon. He was still tying down the tail edge.

"Slim! I come to get a piece of that oilcloth." Slim reached down behind the backboard and threw Midnight a bundle.

"Better move fast, kid. My bones tell me this ain't gonna be just pitter-patter."

"Right." Midnight opened the oilcloth and found a rough hole cut in the middle. He pulled it over his head and took a quick look back at the cattle. They were like one low dark cloud moving slowly toward him. Joe B. and Big Lou waded through the middle, snapping their whips and yelling to move them along.

Midnight spun Dahomey around into the center of the remuda. He popped out his own whip hard.

"Let's go, ponies! Let's move! Come on!" Midnight eased his way to the front and broke Dahomey into a gallop. The other horses followed. Slim's wagon rumbled alongside, then past them. The horses in the remuda seemed to catch on that speed was the thing, because they moved faster. Midnight let Slim keep the lead. He circled back to push the horses from behind. For a moment he looked over at the hills again. The clouds were back, getting darker, and rolling toward them all like loose logs down a mountainside.

They stumbled down into the first gully. The smell of rain floated up from the dust and filled Midnight's nose. Dahomey scrambled up and out of the ditch and Midnight raced to catch up with Slim.

"Slim! What we gonna do when we pass the other gully? Joe B. didn't say—" Fat pellets of rain began to splatter down on the oilcloth.

"Try to ride through the storm! If it gets too bad, we'll stop moving and wait it out!" Slim was yelling now, because the rain was coming fast and hard. It bounced off the backs of the horses. Midnight waved his hand so Slim knew he'd heard. The second gully suddenly appeared, and Midnight hadn't seen it. Dahomey had. He lowered his head toward it. At the same time, Midnight pulled him back. But Dahomey's hooves sank into the muddy slope just as Midnight tightened the reins. The oilcloth blew up over Midnight's face, and he reached up to jerk it down. Dahomey struggled to keep his footing.

"Steady, Dahomey!" Midnight flung off the oilcloth. He loosened his hold on the reins and willed himself to be calm. *If Dahomey and me can't get outta this gully, the other ponies won't either.*

Sheets of rain poured down now, and wind was coming with them. Midnight let Dahomey lead. The horse strained upward. Midnight felt him fighting the mud with each step. Finally they were out on flat ground. Midnight looked back.

The other horses were fighting the mud, too. Rain was collecting in the gully bed, rushing around the horses' sinking hooves. Not far behind, the herd was coming, pushed hard by the crew. The head steers were nearing the first gully at a fast gait, but Big Lou had them under control.

Midnight had to get his horses out of the way. "I'm goin' back, Dahomey." When Midnight slid out of his saddle, the ground underneath his boots was firm. Yet as he started carefully down into the

✳

119

gully, the mud grabbed his heels. Slowly, he lifted one foot, then the other, moving sideways toward two near-crazy horses.

"Calm down, I'm gonna get you out! Somehow." Midnight rested his hand on the nearest animal's heaving flank. She tossed her head at him, pumping her legs to get out. She sank down deeper and deeper.

"Calm, now! Don't fight it." Midnight shook rain from his face and squatted. The mare was almost up to her knees in soft, sticky mud. He dug furiously into the muck, scooping out big handfuls and tossing them aside. The horse sputtered a little, then stood still. *If I only had somethin' more to dig with.* Midnight patted his soggy shirt and his hand hit the steel head of his hammer. He'd forgotten that he'd slung it from his belt when he hurried to free the remuda this morning.

The rain was blowing now. Water began to trickle, then flow around his hands. He dug the claw head of the hammer into the mud, kind of like a spoon. Pushing the mud onto his other hand, he then threw it out of the way. He worked quickly, remembering how he, his mama, and his papa had bent just like this in the cotton fields. They had worked fast, too, but that work never ended. Midnight knew this work would end, and soon.

One leg out. Midnight could hear the cattle coming up behind. *They must be near the first gully. Faster, gotta go faster.* Two legs out. Three. The horse was moving again, trying to climb with her free legs. Four.

"Yo! Get up!" Midnight slapped the horse's rear and watched her scramble up. He pulled his own legs up out of the mud and moved to the other horse. The rain seemed to be lighter now, so the ditch wasn't filling up as fast. Still, the herd was coming. He could feel the ground, muddy as it was, thumping like a heartbeat with the moving of hundreds of hooves. Midnight wiped sweat mixed with rain from his face with a wide open hand. He scooped and remembered . . .

———◆———

Seemed like it happened a lifetime ago. Selling Day was coming up. All the field hands had been working from sunup till sundown. Papa left the field at midday to help tie the cotton into bales and load them onto wagons. Master was hot to make his money, and he decided to leave two days early. The overseer formed a night crew. Papa was on it.

After baling into dark, Papa and five other men were sent back to the field. They picked all night, got a water break, then picked all morning again.

Mama sat up all night, too. "Gonna work my

✳

121

man till he drop! Work him till he sure enough drop!" She never raised her voice, but she kept saying the words over and over. Midnight saw her face at the window, clear by the light of the moon. Mama was tall and lean, her face, her hands, her legs and feet long and narrow. Her skin, like Midnight's, was dark as coffee. Her cheekbones were high, her nose was long and straight. She wore her thick curly hair in small, neat twists over her head. Now Midnight watched that head shake from side to side.

"Mama—" Midnight got up and stood next to her. "Papa's strong. They won't get him down." She touched her fingers on Midnight's arm and leaned against him, just for a minute. Then she stood straight again.

"These people—they care after beasts better than they do us. They feed the cows, they give the horses rest. Do they think we not breathe and feel, too?"

"It's not right—"

"Not right? Not right?" Mama turned to look at him. "It's evil, for sure. And I can't let evil take your papa from us." Midnight started to speak, but Mama put her hand against his lips. He went back to his pallet, but he didn't sleep. *Mama speaks like she's gonna do somethin'*, he thought. He lay with his eyes open until daylight began to glow into the room.

Mama threw open the door of the shack and ran

toward the cotton field. Her bare feet beat small puffs of dust along the path. Midnight followed.

Papa and the other men were stooped in the cotton. The overseer rode up just as Toby, one of the older men, stumbled. Papa reached out his arm to help steady him.

"What you doin', boy? Ain't you got enough to do with your hands?" The overseer cracked his bullwhip and lashed Papa across the shoulder and arm.

"Enough!" Mama shouted, running straight up toward the overseer's horse. The young horse shied away and the man tumbled off. He raised his arm to knock Mama down. Midnight felt a hot anger mixed with fear. Papa jumped from the row and grabbed the man's arm in midair.

"Aw, now!" The angry overseer had gotten his balance back. He elbowed Papa off and swung around with the whip. "Your woman thinks you had enough? I don't!" He flung the whip against Papa's back with a fierce force.

Midnight pulled Mama out of the way of the whip. Over and over it came down on Papa's back. Ten lashes. Twenty. Thirty. Papa staggered, but he stood.

"Johnson!" The master suddenly pulled up in a wagon. "What's wrong with you? That's valuable property there! You kill that slave and you're fired!"

The overseer spun around. Mama broke away

from Midnight and ran to Papa. Midnight rushed behind her. Tears filled his eyes, but he kept blinking them back.

Papa's head was lowered. His hands and arms were swollen and red from the days of picking. Now the skin on his back and shoulders was torn and bloody from the whip. Midnight leaned against one side, Mama the other. Papa draped his heavy arms around their necks.

"Can you walk, Papa?" Midnight whispered.

Papa turned his head to look into Midnight's eyes. Pain and tiredness made his face look sunken in. But his eyes flashed strong and powerful.

"You won't *never* see me on my knees before a man like that, Midnight Son. Never as long as I live." Papa hung heavy on Midnight and Mama, so Midnight knew that he really could just barely stand up. But he did.

thirteen

Midnight was on his knees in the mud. With one more scoop he freed the second horse and stretched to stand. He was up to his ankles in water. The herd was coming fast. He struggled up the side of the gully and whistled for Dahomey. In moments Midnight rounded up the mustangs and galloped out of the way of the coming cattle.

The rain had slowed to a drizzle. The wind still blew. Lightning flashed here and there. Way up ahead Midnight could see a dark shape that he knew was Slim sitting up on the chow wagon. Midnight waved a hand.

"Give me one of them horses, Midnight!" Slim climbed out of the wagon. "I'm gonna help them get the tail of the herd across them gullies."

"But Slim, the rain's slacked up . . . what's

the . . . " Midnight stopped cold. Although the rain was down to a few drips here and there, the sky to the east was so dark it looked black. Swift clouds rolled out of the blackness toward them.

They heard it before they saw it. A dull, far-off roar. Midnight remembered men on the plantation talking about locomotives, the big steam-driven machines that roared along tracks across the land. They said the locomotives made the earth tremble and people cover their ears from the noise.

Midnight looked around crazily. There were no tracks here. No steam puffs shooting into the air. But there was the sound, and it was getting louder and closer. The cattle heard the rumbling, and they began to run wildly in different directions.

"Stampede!" Slim shouted, digging his spurs into his pony. He jerked the pony toward the herd. Midnight stared at the cattle, then realized he'd better get the horses to a safe place. Two low hills came together just north of him. *That could make two sides of a corral,* he thought, yanking his coiled rope from the saddle hook.

"YO!" Midnight drove Dahomey through the middle of the mustangs to lead them. The ponies followed. Then Midnight quickly spun Dahomey around and went back to the opening between the hills, dropping out of his saddle.

"Now, you stay here, Dahomey. Don't go nowhere. Rusty!" The red horse trotted to the front. Midnight led her out, then tied one end of his rope to the trunk of a four-foot-tall scrub bush leaning out of the side of one hill. He stretched the rope across and pounded a picket right into the side of the other hill at about the same level, then tied the other end of the rope to it.

"I'm countin' on you, Dahomey. Stay, boy." Midnight jumped onto Rusty and circled toward the wild cattle. Wind whipped him in the face, almost knocking him off the horse. He held on to the bridle tightly and raced behind Slim. Then he glanced at the sky and his heart jumped up into his throat.

Spinning out from the purple-black clouds was something shaped like a long, stretched-out bell pointing upward and moving fast.

"TWISTER!" Midnight yelled.

"Midnight! Cut off those bulls over there!" Joe B. motioned to three bulls who were hightailing it right toward the coming clouds with some cows behind them. Midnight snapped his whip from his belt and popped it over the frightened longhorn, but they were running for their lives. He rode faster, catching up with them.

"C'mon, Rusty. Let's head 'em off!" Midnight leaned into Rusty's neck and pulled the horse's nose

✳

to the right, heading her right across the lead bull's path. The snorting animal skidded and sidestepped, bumping the others. Midnight kept Rusty close on him, forcing the bulls into a circle move.

"HAA!" Midnight cracked the whip over the racing cows. He waded Rusty among the cattle to stay near the bulls, keeping them moving away from the spinning cloud. Slim, Pablo, Andy, and Lou Boy were nearest to him. They had turned back a few hundred head to join Midnight's group. About a mile back he could see Joe B. and the other hands having a hard time of it ringing the remaining cattle and turning them back.

The wind was getting meaner and the noise louder. Midnight stopped and loosened his bandanna. He quickly folded the corners in till the fabric was one long piece. Then he wrapped the folded bandanna across the top of his hat and pulled the ends together to tie them under his chin.

"What can we do?" he shouted over to Lou Boy.

"Just about nothin'!" Lou Boy shouted back. "These critters could take off again any minute. Best we can do is hold 'em down!" Slim wasn't having that, though. He broke out of the bunch and set out for the others. There was still a distance of nearly a mile between this small group of animals and the larger one. The twister was beating a path straight through the middle.

Slim rode faster. The twister swirled faster. Midnight and Lou Boy watched the twirling clouds kick up brush and bushes and trees. Twigs and dirt blew with the rain, slapping hard against their faces. Everything on the ground below the twister was swept up into the blackness and disappeared. Slim made it across the storm's path just as the spinning tube lifted off the ground and turned roughly.

"Mercy!" Lou Boy raised up out of his saddle. "That thing is changin' direction!"

fourteen

Midnight's mouth fell open. "Slim!" he cried out.

"Pa!" Lou Boy shouted. He forgot the herd and tried to ride out behind the storm. Midnight was with him. But the closeness of the twister had brought more rain and a wind as strong as a wall. The horses wouldn't go against it. The twister had sailed through the air with its tail way up off the ground, yanking off hats as it went. As Midnight and Lou Boy watched helplessly, it started going down.

"No! Pa!" Lou Boy beat his legs against his horse, but the animal wouldn't move.

Midnight whispered to Rusty. "We gotta do somethin', Rusty! Go!"

Rusty only shook her tangled mane and backed away. Not even for her friend would she head for that terrifying sight. Midnight slumped his shoulders. Down, down the cloud spun closer to the ground. The twister's tail dropped to the ground and the whole thing bent forward. First one cow was snatched right off her feet and sucked up into the darkness. Others were picked off, some single and some pairs. Then dozens. The horrible sound the animals made sent a shudder through Midnight's body. He wanted to close his eyes. He tried. But all he could do was blink.

Lou Boy had yelled so that he had no more voice. Midnight grabbed Lou Boy's arm.

The front end of the twister started lifting over the gullies, pulling the air beneath it with a mighty force. Big Lou and his white-maned palomino stood out clearly against the black clouds. Even in the rain the boys could see the horse being lifted, rump first, off the ground.

"PAAAAA!" Lou Boy's wail struck Midnight's heart.

In the blink of an eye, Big Lou and the palomino were gone. The storm lifted higher, pulling its tail through the herd like a sad dog dragging through a farmyard. Slim was caught from behind as he tried to chase a bull out of the way. His horse, too, was jerked up into the air. But the strong, sudden movement threw Slim forty feet and slammed him to the ground somewhere in the wild herd. Just as quickly as it had changed course, the twister snapped up its tail and roared away, dumping sheets of driving rain upon them all.

Midnight was shaking all over. His hand was stuck to Lou Boy's arm. He couldn't make it move.

"Midnight! Lou Boy!" Pablo sped past them. "Stay here. We will round up the rest of the herd, *sí?*" Without waiting for an answer, he and Andy left them.

Midnight swallowed. He realized that he was able to move. His throat felt as if the flying twigs had scraped his insides raw. He fumbled for his water gourd, then looked down to see that it was long gone. He patted his chest for the little pouch Papa had given him. It was still there, a soaking wet wad of fabric wrapped around the Mexican coins. He ran his hand across the back of his saddle for Miss Miracles' blanket. It was still tied tightly down against the leather.

The rain was hard but it didn't last. It raced along behind the twister. The noise went, too, becoming fainter and fainter as the storm sailed into the sky and out of sight. Left behind was a gray sky, water-soaked earth, and disaster. The bodies of steers and cows lay around among uprooted trees. It looked like a giant had thrown them away.

"Lou Boy?" Midnight found his voice. It sounded strange, shaky, but it was his voice.

Lou Boy turned his wet face to Midnight. Every ounce of color he'd had in it had drained away. His eyes were empty.

"Lou Boy," Midnight repeated. Lou Boy's body was shaking, too.

"Help me count how many head we got left here," Midnight said. "Joe B.'ll want to know. Soon as we get this done, we can go look for Big Lou."

Lou Boy looked at Midnight. Now there was feeling in his eyes. Tears were there. Sadness was there. And a loneliness that Midnight knew very well.

"Ain't no use lookin', Midnight. You saw. I saw."

Midnight nodded slowly. The two of them looked off in the direction that the storm had gone, but there was nothing left.

"I saw," Midnight whispered, half to himself. *And I'll never forget it.*

It took hours more to round up and count the surviving cattle and patch up the men. Big Lou was, indeed, gone forever. They couldn't find anything left of him—not his hat, a boot, his lariat—nothing. Slim had been bruised badly by cattle hooves. He'd broken his left arm. "Not my cookin' arm," he said. Kid had been knocked out cold by a flying tree limb, but he came to with a big headache later. The other men had cuts and scrapes. Midnight had finally gone back to check on his horses. All had made it. Since the storm had traveled in another direction, his "corral" had been tight enough to stand the wind, and the horses hadn't strayed.

It was nightfall by the time the crew and what was left of the herd had settled down. Slim's chow wagon was a tangled mess of soggy sacks and dented tin cups and bowls. His prized barrel of molasses was split and empty. Most of the flour was wet and ruined. Somehow he found his cast-iron skillet and coffeepot. He managed to throw together some coffee and hoecake before his damp fire fizzled out. That, and some dried beef jerky, was what he served up for the bone-tired men. They had already started gulping down the food when Joe B. cleared his throat and stood up beside Slim.

"Wait a minute, fellas. I wanna talk about Big Lou." All the men lowered their cups. Lou Boy shifted in his spot near the fire.

"Big Lou Holt was a hardworking man. Never walked away from a tough fight, never turned his back on a friend. Big Lou and Slim and me met up about ten years ago, when Big Lou was farming in Indian territory. Lou Boy was just a puppy back then. When Big Lou's wife died five years ago, he looked me up. Said he wanted to start over. He was my right hand." Joe B. looked right at Lou Boy. "He was a good man, and, believe me, the Lord is gettin' the best cattle-roper I ever seen!" Joe B. smiled. Slim nodded.

Midnight looked at Lou Boy. Lou Boy was staring at him. Midnight dropped his eyes to the muddy ground.

"Now." Joe B.'s word brought all their heads up, brought their coffee cups and bread back to their mouths. "By my count, we lost five hundred sixty head, give or take ten. I guess it coulda been worse. Food supply was pretty much wiped out, Slim says. There's a way station and a store in Abilene. So we'll lay on enough supplies to get us into Wyandotte. We didn't lose any horses, on account of the quick thinking of Midnight Son. If it hadn't been for him, we couldn't even get to Abilene."

Joe B. looked at Midnight. "Two days' rest and we've gotta move. I don't wanna run into Indians after all we been through already." He turned away from them all, hunching his big shoulders and walking into the chilly night. Midnight got up. He sat down next to Lou Boy. For a while neither of them said anything.

"I feel bad about your papa." Midnight spoke quietly. "I ain't got no wise words or nothin'." He stopped, trying to find some.

"Seems like since we saw . . . saw what happened together, now we're bound to each other some kinda

✳

135

way." He paused again. "I-I don't know what I'm sayin'."

Lou Boy moved his foot, making a swirling pattern in the mud. Even in the dark, they could both see it.

"What you're sayin' is you're my friend now."

"Is that what I'm sayin'? That demon storm made us friends?"

"No, fool. You know what I mean." Lou Boy lifted one side of his mouth in a half-smile. Midnight returned it with a full one.

"Yeah, yeah. You and me shared 'bout the most awful thing that can happen to a pa and his boy. 'Cause of that, I got my first white friend." Midnight slapped Lou Boy on the back. Lou Boy stopped smiling. His voice was serious.

"Thanks, Midnight." The ground crackled behind them. Midnight looked up to see Curly standing, fiddling with his coffee cup.

"Um . . . pardon me . . . Louis . . ."

"Louis?" Midnight raised his eyebrows. Lou Boy paid him no attention.

"Yeah, Curly."

"I wanna pay my respects about your da. My da passed away when I was a lad. I'm sorry." Lou Boy shook his head, but didn't look up. Midnight figured he should leave. As he rose, Curly touched his arm.

"I'm sorry to you, too."

" 'Bout what?" Midnight looked at him hard.

"I thought before that there weren't nothin' behind you but hot air. After that cat and all, I thought you was just a show-off. But I judged you wrong, Midnight Son." He looked straight at him. This time, Midnight looked at him, grabbed his hand, and shook it. Then he walked away.

fifteen

One week later, Joe B. led Slim, Midnight, and Curly through the tiny village of Abilene. They passed a few mud-roofed houses and stopped at a small wooden building. A few men were gathered on the porch outside. They stared hard at the group of ragged cowboys, but none spoke. Joe B. pushed through the door and the others followed. Midnight wished he had eyes in the back of his head.

Got a feelin' some of these folk ain't too eager to do business with the likes of me and Slim. Joe B. went on and did his business. He stacked up gold coins and they walked out with a sack of flour, a barrel of salt pork, and a sack of beans. Midnight and Curly carried the supplies out. Slim and Joe B. flanked them, their hands on their guns.

Curly muttered to Midnight, "It ain't the farmers

they're worried about, y'know. Anybody starts talkin' that they saw gold money, and robbers will be upon us before we get back to the herd!"

They did get back. Slim cooked beans and biscuits that night. After another ten days, they drove what was left of the herd into Wyandotte.

✻ ✻ ✻

All those things happened to me; now I'm in Wyandotte, Kansas, with gold pieces in my pocket! Midnight had rented a small, clean room in Miss Ellen's Boarding House. Joe B. had told him that it was a nice, quiet place. He'd said Midnight would have no problems there—she took in anybody who didn't make trouble, no matter what color they were. Midnight looked around . . . white curtains at the window . . . big brass bed . . . polished wood dresser. . . . There was a knock on the door.

"Yeah?" Midnight turned.

"It's your bath, mister!"

Midnight opened the door to see a wiry little brown boy carrying a tin tub twice his size. Their eyes met just over the rim.

"Gee—" The boy put the tub down and threw Midnight two big white towels. "You with that outfit that came in today?" He leaned in the doorway, all eight years of him.

"Yeah." Midnight smiled.

"I seen black cowpokes before, but none young as you." He shoved out his small hand. "I'm Bill."

"I'm Midnight."

"I bet you got some great yarns to tell about that drive! Didja run into Injuns? Didja herd stampede? How come you got to be a cowboy? You're just a kid, like me!" Midnight laughed out loud. *He sounds like me, only I never had the nerve to ask what I wanted to know. 'Sides, nobody was gonna give no slave kid the time of day.*

"I'm a cowpoke 'cause I used to be a slave, and my papa and mama helped me run. Now I'm on my own."

Bill looked at Midnight with more wonder. "You was a slave? My mama says that's a wicked business."

"Your mama is sure 'nuff right. You musta been born free, huh?" Bill shook his head yes. Then he seemed to remember that he was supposed to be working.

"Oh. I'll be bringing up your hot water right away."

"Never mind," Midnight told him. Bill looked Midnight up and down.

"What you gonna do for clothes after you have your bath?"

Midnight hadn't thought of that. He dropped his

eyes to his mud-caked pants and torn shirt. Bill clucked like a hen.

"I could run out and get you some new duds. Ain't gonna cost much. My ma's got a laundry business. I could get some secondhands for cheap."

Midnight thought about his pouch of money, but he didn't touch it yet. He had always dreamed of having money, of spending money. Now that he had some, he didn't like the idea of parting with it so fast. *Sure, I could go bustin' out with new clothes. For what? Who've I got to show off for? I'll just get what I need and wait to spread my money around.*

"All right, Bill. I'll take your offer. Gimme two shirts and a pair of pants."

"And them boots?" Bill frowned down at them. "How about some new ones?"

Midnight sat on the bed and stuck out his feet. *Juan Diego Sanchez Rivera is in these boots. I can't never give them up.* He tugged them off.

"I'm kinda partial to these," he said. "Could you get 'em cleaned up and polished for me? I'll pay extra for that."

Bill scooped up the boots. "I'll do 'em myself," he said.

Midnight reached into his pouch. He carefully picked out three coins. "This oughta cover it all." Bill nodded.

"And, if you want a good hot meal, try Aunt Lil's place in back of the Trail's End Hotel. She's my cousin. Best hoecake north of the South!" He grinned.

"Aw, shucks! You kin to everybody in this town, Bill?" Midnight threw a towel at the closing door and fell back on the bed. *There's somethin' sweet about spendin' my first money with somebody like me. Feels real good.*

Bill brought the hot water faster than Midnight expected. He brought it by the bucketful. *A bath! We only got baths once a year back at Greely's place. Don't remember none at Sampson's. Rest of the time we had to wash up at the creek, or cart water and heat it in the cabins to clean our own bodies. Ha! Now I can get myself clean— really clean—anytime I want. This is nice.*

While Midnight was soaking in the tub, Bill came back with two crisp white shirts that looked like new. The heavy pants were just what he needed on the trail. On top of the stack were two pairs of socks. By the time Midnight had scrubbed and dressed, Bill brought his boots. The sunlight from the window bounced off the shine. Bill set them down carefully.

✳

"Everything okay?" he asked. "I got your change." He opened his palm to show Midnight the silver coins.

"Keep it, Bill. Thanks for everything." Bill touched his forehead in a funny, soldier kind of move and left. Midnight had washed his bandanna and laid it out to dry. He tied it on now and picked up his hat.

Aunt Lil's wasn't hard to find. It was really just a small room at the back of a small hotel. When Midnight got there it was crowded with all kinds of men. Black, white, Indian, Mexican men. Midnight looked around through the cigar and pipe smoke for an empty seat. At a corner table, he saw Lou Boy sitting alone.

"How 'bout some company?"

"Slim says the food here is good as his," Lou Boy told him.

They both ordered baked chicken and mashed potatoes. The food came. They ate without talking. A round, honey-brown woman brought two thick slices of wonderful-smelling cake.

"Watcha gonna do next?" Lou Boy asked.

"Eat my cake."

"Naw, you know what I mean. Joe B. asked me to come back to the Crazy Eight. I dunno if I can go back. Where you goin'?"

Midnight shifted in his seat. He had tried for as long as he could to put off thinking about the end of the drive. But now, here it was. He wasn't sure he

✳

wanted to stay in Wyandotte County. It seemed a little too busy. He didn't feel safe about the idea of traveling alone, not yet.

"I ain't decided. Lou Boy, this was the best time of my life. This was my dream, to roam free under the sun and sky. The drive is finished. Don't that mean that my dream is finished, too?" Before Lou Boy could answer, a voice they both knew butted into the conversation.

sixteen

"Well, now . . . That's a sorry dream if one trail drive finishes it off!" Slim dragged over a chair with one hand. The other arm was bandaged up in a sling. Everything he wore was new: fancy straw hat, blue shirt, black vest, pants, tall black boots. He even had new silver spurs.

"Slim!"

"Sit down!"

"Don't mind if I do." He reared back in his chair toward the kitchen. "Hey, Lillian! Lemme see how you damaged my pound cake recipe!" He laughed heartily. Then he looked from Midnight to Lou Boy. He sensed that they didn't feel so much like laughing.

✳

145

"Fellas, this was a rough ride. Lou, you had the worst of it for sure. But Big Lou never stopped livin' after he lost your ma, did he?" Lou Boy dropped his head. Slim turned to Midnight.

"And you, free man. Ain't your will to live outside of bondage bigger than one trail drive? Lookit the two of you! Cryin' in your coffee!"

Midnight tossed his head up. "You can talk big, Slim! You got a family to go back to. We ain't got nothin'." Slim leaned forward and banged his good hand on the table. The dishes rattled.

"Midnight, I declare! You got your freedom. Use it. Lou Boy, you got everything your pa taught you. That's plenty. I'm an old man. This is the end for me. You two got youth and strength. Don't waste it." Midnight chewed slowly.

"I reckon I gotta make some choices," he mumbled.

Slim shifted his bandaged arm. "I'm ridin' back to Rio Gatos. You're both welcome to go as far as Hacienda de la Suerte with me."

Midnight pushed away from the table, leaving money beside his plate.

"I-I need some time. See y'all later."

Midnight wandered outside. All over town cowboys were spending their pay. He passed saloons where he could see rowdy card games going on. Music shouted out from many of the places, and men who'd had too much drink stumbled around. Midnight walked to the stable where Dahomey was boarded.

"Hello, boy." Midnight climbed into his saddle and rode. He passed the buildings, the people, the noise. Soon he was out in the countryside again. He breathed deeply.

"Yo! Get on up!" Dahomey stretched his neck and ran. They rode for hours. Midnight wanted the air to clear his mind. Instead, the last year danced in his head.

I'm like a fish out of water, floppin' around on the creek bank. I wanted to be on my own, and I am. No one to tell me what to do 'cept me. Only thing missin' is having someplace to go home to at the end of the drive. But I wanna ride. I wanna do this again and again. Midnight had decided.

Joe B. didn't hold with the life in town, so he kept camp on the outskirts. Midnight rode up on Dahomey just as all the hands had gathered around the fire.

"Midnight!"

"Doin' some night ridin'?"

"What brings you here?" Joe B. pointed Midnight to a spot between Andy and Pablo. They were swigging homemade beer and telling tales. Midnight sat and looked around at their faces. Even Slim and Lou Boy were there. Their chatter stopped; they all seemed to be waiting for him to speak. Midnight guessed that Slim and Lou Boy had been talking to the others about him. He

✳

147

could've felt angry, but at least they cared. *Might as well get it right out.*

"Joe B., I want a job on the Crazy Eight, if you'll have me."

Joe B. looked into the fire, rubbing on his stubble of a beard. "Jake is leaving to join a crew in Denver. Lone Eagle is going back to his people for a while. Slim . . ." He cut his eyes at his silver-haired friend. "Slim has made up his mind to live the quiet life." The men broke up into whoops and hollers.

"So I reckon I need to shore up my new crew for my drive next spring."

Midnight sat up. "You plannin' another drive?"

"That's how I work, Midnight. We go back, raise a herd, I make a deal, we drive 'em up for sale. I'm no farmer. I'm a rancher. And you're no kid. You're a cowboy." Joe B. stretched his hand out. Midnight leaned out and pumped it hard. He looked at Lou Boy.

"I'm goin' back too." Lou Boy smiled that half-smile. Midnight sat back on his haunches. Through the flickering firelight Slim smiled slyly at him.

"Hey, Jake, remember that tune Andy came up with after the bobcat fight?" The men started laughing as Jake pulled out his fiddle. Midnight rolled his eyes.

"Well, I got me some new words to put to it. Play!

Way back in the mean old West,
Lived a brave young cowboy who was one of the best.
He was Africa and America rolled into one;
He was the cowboy called . . . Midnight Son!"

Midnight made one last pass through Wyandotte. He ate a meal at Aunt Lil's, then searched for the laundry that Bill's mama owned. He ended up following a trail of steam behind some sheds near the livery stable.

Four great big cauldrons sat boiling upon fire pits dug in the ground. Clotheslines hung crisscrossed over the alley. Two girls stirred the cauldrons with long, heavy sticks.

" 'Scuse me—I'm lookin' for Bill."

"He's inside." One of the girls pointed her elbow toward an open door. Midnight went in. There Bill was, stacking freshly pressed shirts into a big basket. Standing near him over a makeshift ironing board was a tall, yellow-skinned woman with brown hair piled up on her head. She looked up at Midnight and wiped her hands on her apron.

"Can I help ya?"

Bill's head snapped up. He climbed over the basket. "Ma! This is Midnight!"

Bill's mama raised one of her eyebrows. "Oh, you the one who's been filling Billy's head with notions of joining up with a crew?"

Midnight looked at Bill. Bill's face turned red. "No, ma'am. I'm the one who was tellin' Bill how lucky he is to be born a free man." Bill's mother's eyebrow went down. She glanced sideways at Bill.

"Well, he's not a man yet. And when he is, I hope he remembers just what you said. I see those clothes fit you nicely." She smiled and reached out her hand. "I'm Bea Dixon."

"Yes, ma'am. I reckon you know my name's Midnight Son. Thank you for the duds. I'm here to say my good-byes."

"Good-bye, son. You carry yourself proud. Keep on." Bill's mother turned to her hot stove and wrapped the tail of her apron around a hot iron handle. Midnight watched her pick up the iron and slap it down on a wrinkled wet shirt. Steam shot up around her as she slid the iron over the shirt, pressing the wrinkles out smooth.

"See ya, Midnight." Bill walked out with him to the edge of the alley and watched him ride away.

I hope I can always carry myself proud, Midnight thought. *Mama told me to be strong. Seems like those two, proud and strong, go together. Wish Mama could see me now.*

Midnight's eyes fell on a store window that he hadn't paid attention to before. It was a general store, and the window was mostly filled with horse gear and farm supplies. In one corner, draped over a barrel, was what Midnight was looking at. He hitched Dahomey and went inside.

"May I help you?" A woman came over to the counter.

"That ribbon in the window," Midnight said. He nervously shifted his weight from one foot to the other. The woman pulled out three big rolls. She spun the shimmering red and blue and green satin across the dark wood. Midnight looked at it in wonder. He touched a finger to the red and drew it back, quickly, as if it was red-hot.

"Can I have some? I mean, can I buy some?"

"Surely." The woman wore a pair of scissors on a cord around her neck. "How much would you like?" she asked, holding her scissors in the air.

"Uh . . ."

"One yard? Two yards? May I ask if it's for a young lady's hair?"

Midnight looked at her. "Yes."

"Then may I suggest two yards of each?"

"Sounds good." Midnight watched her roll out the ribbon against a measuring stick. She cleanly cut each color. Then she rolled the ribbon and wrapped it in brown paper. Midnight paid her and put the small package into his special pouch.

That spendin' felt even better than buyin' the clothes from

Bill's mama. I don't know when, and I don't know how, but this prettiness is gonna end up in Truth and Queen's hands. They're gonna know what freedom feels like, too, Grandma Femi. I promise.

He was late, he knew. Joe B. and the others were waiting a few miles out of town. Midnight patted the pouch and spurred Dahomey into a canter past the rest of Wyandotte. The shining new train rails stretched alongside them, running into the distance as far as Midnight could see.

I gotta lay my eyes on a locomotive one day. Wonder if somebody like me, born slave, could ever ride that thing the same as somebody free born? Go from one end of this country to the other? I'll bet. Might just be me!

"Yo!" Midnight sang out. "Yip! Yip! Get on up!" Dahomey stretched his big black head and galloped off. He and Midnight were one. Moving like the wind.